# McCabe's Luck

# Also by Patrick Lindsay

*Opening the Frontier: Spencer and Son*

*Texas Rangers Stone & McKinnon*

## Chance Reilly Series

*Chance Reilly*

*Gibson's Gold*

*Agua Caliente Canyon*

## Latigo Series

*Latigo's Choice: Taming the West*

*Latigo's Chance: Boomtown Gold*

*Latigo's Trouble: Meltdown in Leadville*

# McCabe's Luck

## Jake McCabe
### Book One

## Patrick Lindsay

WOLFPACK
PUBLISHING
— EST 2013 —

# McCabe's Luck

# CHAPTER 1

## CORNERED

L ate spring days can be hot in the northeastern Kentucky hills, and I was feeling every bit of the heat. It didn't help that I was lying flat on my stomach in the underbrush, my face and hands being scratched by thorns and twigs. I didn't dare raise my head to get my bearings. The last time I'd tried, two bullets had whizzed past my head and buried themselves in the maple trees behind me. Even moving around to ease the pain in my back and legs brought a fresh fusillade of bullets into my area. I couldn't even be sure how many of them were out there. What I knew for sure was that they wanted to kill me.

I managed to roll to my right to take shelter behind a thick tree trunk. The movement brought a couple of searching shots from the trees across the stream in front of me, but they weren't coming as close this time. I tried to gather my thoughts and make sense of the situation I found myself in. I had gone on a brief hunting trip. Only my younger brother and I lived in the old family cabin.

Neither of our parents were still alive, so it was just the two of us in the cabin. My mother had died giving birth to my younger brother. My dad had signed up for the Union army when I did. I had survived the battle at Shiloh, but my dad hadn't been so lucky. They had pinned his unit down in the fighting at the Hornet's Nest area on that first bloody day of battle. Relief troops came too late to help him. Dad was one of many buried at that battlefield.

I had come home after the war, almost eight years ago, at age twenty-two. I hadn't been made to feel very welcome when I came home, and now, at age thirty, things didn't seem any different in that regard. Kentucky was supposed to be a neutral state, but where I lived, nearly everyone else had joined the Confederate army. Only one family near us will let bygones be bygones. My younger brother Russell was a peaceful man who hadn't fought on either side. He wanted only to be left alone—to live his life in peace. Increasing hostility from the surrounding people, particularly the Mueller clan, had made that much harder these days. Russell had gotten to the point where he barely wanted to leave the cabin. I'm a calm man with a slow fuse, but I don't have quite as peaceful nature as my brother. Today's attack was the last straw for me.

My name is Jake McCabe, and I have mostly known hard times. Today looked to be another of those hard times. I had been riding back to the cabin, and I estimated I was about two or three miles away from it when a rifle shot rang out. The shot had notched a tree next to me, close enough that my cheek was bleeding from the tree bark torn off by the shot. I hadn't survived four years in the army without developing some survival instincts. I had grabbed my Spencer carbine from the scabbard and had thrown myself on the ground, then crawled in to the thickest underbrush I could find. I estimated that maybe nine or ten shots had followed that first one. My horse lay dead on the ground behind me.

I lay flat on the ground and studied the woods in front of me. I had to get a better idea of how many of them were out there, and where they were. I pulled a long tree branch toward me very slowly, then pulled off my old Union army cap and cut a small hole in it. Then, I placed it over a twig at the end of the branch. I pushed the branch back away from me slowly, then lifted it up above the cover of the underbrush, watching the ground in front of me carefully. Three puffs of smoke appeared almost simultaneously, accompanied by the sound of rifle shots. They tore the hat off the branch and sailed into the bushes behind me. The smoke puffs had been grouped close together. If they had been smart, they would have spread out and bracketed me a lot better. Then again, of course, nobody had ever accused those Mueller boys of being smart. And I had a feeling I was dealing with the Mueller boys.

I had seen a bit of color, maybe somebody's shirt, showing from the spot farthest to my left when the smoke puffs had appeared. I thought I had a pretty good bead on that position. I crawled a little farther to my left to position myself behind a fallen log. Then I laid the Spencer across the log, sighting in on where I'd seen that color. I grabbed a rock lying on the ground beside me and tossed it over into the underbrush at about the spot where I'd raised my hat. I saw color again as he came off the ground and presented me with a target while he fired. I took aim and squeezed off my shot. He pitched over backward and his rifle fell into the brush behind him. I shifted the rifle and fired one shot each into the other two places where I had seen the smoke. I heard a scream coming from the center position, then pressed myself down behind the log when they sent answering rifle fire just over my head. I was pretty sure there was only one gun now, returning my fire.

I could see the second man I'd hit crawling on the ground, trying to reach the rise at the top of the stream bank. It was one of the Mueller brothers, just as I had thought. I could see from here, about fifty yards away, that he was bleeding pretty badly. I let him go. My army experience told me that with the size of the blood trail he was leaving, he probably wouldn't last out the day. I glanced over and could see the feet and legs of the first man I had shot, lying in the underbrush. He hadn't moved since landing in that position. I was pretty sure he was dead. The third brother broke from his concealed spot in the brush and ran up the slope toward his wounded brother, who had almost reached the top of the rise. That last brother foolishly stopped running, turned, and lifted his rifle to take one more try at me. I dropped him with one shot.

I stayed where I was for a while, not willing to expose my position, just in case there was anybody else out there. After about fifteen minutes, I stood and walked back to my horse. I pulled off my saddlebags, then looked at the deer carcass I had strapped on the horse, glancing overhead after a moment. The buzzards were already circling up there. I pulled out my knife and took a few small cuts of venison, wrapping them up in a cloth and pushing them into my saddlebags. Then I turned and started walking to the cabin.

My family settled on our little piece of land in Kentucky when I was only about one year old, before my brother Russell was born. We had struggled to make a go of it. We'd been flooded out once, burned out twice, and had suffered several years of poor crops and hunger. Folks around here had taken to calling it McCabe's luck. The feud with the Muellers had started when the four of them, including old Ezra Mueller, the father, had enlisted in the Confederate army. Dad and I had marched off to join Sherman's troops, and there were some hard feelings. Until now, it hadn't been deadly. Once in a while, one of our pigs or chickens turned up missing, and we were pretty sure the Mueller boys were taking them. Day before yesterday, I had seen somebody making off with one chicken and had fired a warning shot just over his head. Maybe that had set them off.

I walked reluctantly, forcing myself to keep up the pace. I had to get home and find out if they had targeted Russell and the cabin as well. When I had gone only about a mile, I crested a small rise and saw what I had feared from the minute the Mueller boys had ambushed me back there. There was a column of smoke rising into the sky from our cabin site.

———

I could see Russell's body lying in the center of the clearing around the cabin just as soon as I rounded the turn on the trail. I broke into a shambling trot, not really wanting to see what I knew had happened. They had shot Russell in the back, probably while he was trying to reach the cabin to get his rifle. I turned him over gently, checked him quickly, then sat in the dust next to Russell, my face buried in my hands. I didn't seem to have any tears. Behind me, I could hear the flames still licking at the remains of the cabin.

After a while, I stood and walked to the edge of the clearing around the cabin, my hands stuffed into my pockets. I stared out into the woods. They must have come here first, looking for both of us. When they had finished here, they'd probably hidden out in the woods near the trail, waiting for me to come home. They probably hadn't waited very long. I stood there for a long time, then eventually, I walked around to the small garden we kept behind the house. We didn't really have a tool shed. A shovel and a hoe lay on the ground next to the garden. I picked up the shovel, walked back around to the clearing, and began digging the grave.

I supposed I was all that was left of either family involved in this senseless feud. Both my parents and my brother were gone now, and I didn't think any of the Muellers had been left alive. Old Ezra Mueller had died in the war, and his wife had died shortly after hearing the news of Ezra's death. The three no-account brothers were the only ones left from their family, and I was pretty sure all three were dead after today's ambush attempt. I didn't even plan to go back and give them a burial.

I finished the grave and laid Russell to rest. I took off my hat and said a few words over him, filled in the grave and rigged a little headstone for him. That done, I didn't plan to stay here for even one more day. There was nothing to keep me here now.

I walked back around the old cabin site, giving it a wide berth because of the heat from the flames and ashes. One glance told me there was nothing I could recover from inside the cabin. I tossed the shovel back into the garden, then followed a narrow trail back into the woods. Russell had been a very mistrusting man where most of his neighbors were concerned, for good reason, as it turned out. He had left me two parting gifts.

I followed the twisting trail for about a half mile until it ended in a small clearing. We had built a little makeshift corral in the clearing where we kept our best horse, a sorrel with a white blaze. I had named him Sherman. I didn't think General Sherman would mind having a horse named after him. He was a pretty good horse, after all. Sherman whinnied as I walked over. I rubbed his ears, but left him where he was for a moment. I turned and walked back to a fairly large rock at the edge of the trail, then bent and heaved the rock to one side. I scooped out the dirt underneath with my hands for about a minute until I felt the tin can we had buried there.

I scooped away the last few handfuls of dirt and pulled the can from the ground. I turned it over and dumped the contents into the clearing. Fifteen twenty-dollar gold pieces spilled out of the can and came to rest on the ground. I picked them up and tucked them away in my pockets. They were going to be my grubstake to allow me to move away and leave this place behind me. Maybe with a new home, I could change the bad luck the McCabes had found here.

I went back over to get Sherman and led him to a tarp we had stretched over two piles of logs. In the space between the logs were a blanket, bridle and saddle. After I saddled Sherman, I mounted and rode him back down the trail. I paused for a moment beside Russell's grave, then turned away from the scene of this morning's ambush and rode down the trail toward the one family I wanted to see before I left this place.

The Hawkins family comprised most of the people I counted as friends in this little corner of northeastern Kentucky. We'd never been the most popular people around, but the choice I'd made to join the Union army seemed to end all the friendships I had around here. With the exception of the Hawkins family. Ike Hawkins had served in the Confederate army. He had lost a leg early on and had come home to his family. He had never held it against me or my father that we had chosen the other side. He simply said that a man had to do what he believes is the right thing to do. His wife, Jeanne, was a withdrawn, quiet woman. The last several years must have been hard on her, because she seemed to pull back farther and farther from other people.

There were two boys—Pete, about sixteen years old, and Isaac, maybe fourteen. They were friendly, respectful, hard-working boys. They had come over to our cabin a time or two to help Russell and me when there was a lot of work to be done. It was the daughter in the family, though, that I thought was special. Julia Hawkins was about five years younger than me, and I had ridden over to see her often. The family made it clear that my feet were welcome under their dinner table, and Julia never failed to send me home with something special she had baked for me. I thought she understood me better than probably anybody I knew.

I wondered for about the fiftieth time if I shouldn't have pushed for something more with Julia. I had always felt that a man needed more to offer a woman than what

I had to offer Julia. The smoking ruin of a shack back there and the little piece of ground we called home didn't seem like much of a future to offer a woman. I sighed and nudged Sherman around the last little turn in the trail. It was too late to worry about that now. I had come to say goodbye to all of them.

Ike Hawkins stood in the doorway when I rode up, leaning on his crutch. It wasn't lost on me that he held his rifle at his side. I wasn't too sure how well he could shoot with that since he'd lost his leg, but I wouldn't want to be the one who put him to the test. He gave me a brief wave and surveyed the trail behind me.

"Saw some smoke over your way," he said as I dismounted and walked up to the door. I nodded and stared at the ground as the rest of the family gathered behind him in the doorway.

"Russell's dead. The cabin's been burned down," I told them. I heard a collective gasp, and they stood aside to let me inside.

I sat down on the fireplace hearth, and Julia came to sit beside me while I told them about the ambush, and how I had found Russell dead and the cabin burned. I finished by telling them that I felt sure I had killed two of the Mueller brothers, and most likely all three. There was a long silence.

"You did what you had to do," Ike finally offered. I nodded mutely.

They asked me to join them for a meal, and I accepted, mainly because I needed the company. I didn't do the food justice like I usually did. I picked at it for a short while before finally pushing it away. They all offered to come over and help me rebuild the cabin, and I said nothing for quite a while.

Finally, in the long silence that followed, Julia leaned over and asked: "What will you do now, Jake?" My eyes traveled slowly around the table, taking in each of them. I didn't seem to be able to say what I needed to. Finally, I looked back around at Julia.

"Can I talk to you outside?" I asked her.

# CHAPTER 2

## UPROOTED

We sat on an old bench in front of the Hawkins house. Julie folded her hands in her lap and waited for me to talk. I shifted back and forth in my seat, clearing my throat a couple times without getting started. She helped me after a moment.

"The Muellers are all gone," she started. "There's no feud to continue now."

I glanced up and nodded. "I know," I said, "but my family hasn't been very popular around here ever since the war, and the Muellers had quite a few friends. I..." I lapsed into silence, trying to finish the thought in my own head. "I don't know how much sense it makes to start out again around here," I said finally. "Maybe things could go better for me somewhere else."

Julia looked down at her hands. "I guess that makes sense," she said in a low voice. "Where would you go?" That was something I had been turning over in my head, and I didn't have a suitable answer yet—just a vague idea I'd had on the way over.

"They're doing pretty well down in Texas," I began. "They're running cattle up to Kansas and selling them. I don't think I want to do that, but there's money down there because of it. Better chance down there than around here." I looked up to see how Julia was taking this. To my surprise, there was a light in her eyes and a little smile on her face.

"Wait here," she told me, then ran into the house.

She returned with what appeared to be a newspaper article she had cut out and saved. I looked at the top of the article and saw that the newspaper was named the *Austin Weekly Democratic Statesman*. The date was a day in this month, April 1872. I looked up at her, surprised, and she just shrugged.

"My cousin sent it to me," she told me. I looked back down and began to read. The article was titled *Confederate Scrip Program*. I read through it once, then went back to the top and began to read again. The part that caught my attention said, "To persons who have been permanently disabled by reason of wounds received while in the service of this State, or of the Confederate States, a land certificate for twelve hundred and eighty acres of land."

I gave her a surprised look for the second time, and she was smiling at me this time. I looked back at the qualification for this land grant. The person must be disabled—Ike was certainly that and had been injured while serving in the Confederate army. I read the other items. Only one seemed to be a problem.

"It says," I told her, "that you must have two people who can state that you are a resident of the state."

She stared off into the woods. "Maybe," she said hesitantly, "if somebody went down there ahead of us and got a place where we could live for a while, we could go in after a few months and get the land." She glanced at me sideways.

I stared. Several thoughts came to mind, only to be crowded out by other thoughts. "I have nothing to offer," I started, then stopped. "I don't..."

Julia moved a little closer on the bench. "The land would be free," she pointed out. "If you went down there, found out a little more about the program and helped us move in somewhere long enough to be citizens, it would help us out a lot. Maybe you could..." Now it was her turn for her voice to trail away. An awkward silence ensued.

"What about your family?" I asked finally. "Are they aware of this idea? Would they go along?"

Julia glanced toward the house. "I'm sure my brothers would be all for it," she said. "And I think Dad would, too. Mother...is pretty hesitant about most things, but I think Dad would talk her into it." She stood and tugged at my sleeve. "There's one way to find out," she told me.

I trailed behind Julia into the house, then watched the family file into the main room at her request. She held the newspaper clipping in her hand, waving it around a few times while she told the family she would like each one of them to read the article, then talk about it. Ike settled himself in the big chair at the corner of the room, his one good leg extended awkwardly in front of him. His wife, Jeanne, sat in the other chair next to him. Julia stood across the room near the fireplace, and the two boys took a seat against one wall. I seated myself on the floor near the fireplace and waited while Ike slowly read the newspaper clipping.

He read it through slowly, then appeared to read

through it again. He glanced up at Julia, a small smile on his face, then passed it to his wife without comment. Jeanne skimmed it, opened her mouth as if to say something, then passed it to the older boy without comment. Pete's face lit up when he read it, as did his brother Isaac's face. Isaac stood, crossed the room, gave the clipping to Julia, then returned to take a seat against the wall. Everybody looked at Ike.

Ike leaned back and looked down at his one good leg, then looked up. "Well," he said, "I can't do everything I used to be able to do, but I could still milk cows, mend fences and other things." He looked over at the boys. "These kids could have a better future, some land to call their own. I like it a lot." He looked over at his wife, who hesitated, then glanced around.

"Is it safe there?" she asked. She looked at me.

"I don't know, ma'am," I answered honestly. "But I'm about to go down there and find out." She shifted her gaze to Julia.

"It says we have to be residents of Texas," she pointed out.

Julia glanced over at me, and I nodded my agreement with what I knew she was about to say. "Jake can help us out with that, I think," she said. Several glances shifted in my direction. I stood up, but let her continue. "As Jake just said, he has decided to move down to Texas for a fresh start," she said. "He has agreed he can look for a small piece of land for the family to live on, and might find out more about this land program for veterans. We could move down there and live on that land for a while, and when we've been there long enough to become residents, we could get the grant."

Jeanne had one more question: "Did you have to fight for Texas troops, or just for the Confederacy?"

Julia looked at the clipping one more time. "It says, 'this State, or the Confederate States,'" she pointed out. Ike shifted in his chair.

"My unit was so decimated at Shiloh, they put us in with Hood's division on the second day," he told us. "I fought with both the Texas boys and the unit from Kentucky."

A quick glance around the room told me that this idea was a winner. Ike was smiling, and the two boys were absolutely beaming. Jeanne looked a bit hesitant, but she was clearly being outvoted. "I love it," boomed Ike. He looked at me. "Texas is a big place. Any idea where in Texas you would look for the land?" I gathered my thoughts for a moment, then shrugged. "I guess I'm open for ideas," I admitted. "Julia and I only started talking about this about a half hour ago."

Ike rose slowly to his feet, walked over to Jeanne and conferred with her in low tones for a couple of minutes. She then nodded slowly, and Ike made his way on his crutch to a small desk in a corner of the room. He pulled open a drawer, pulled out a small bag, and I heard the noise of coins clinking on the desk. He swept up some coins and put them back in the bag. He returned the rest of the coins to the desk drawer, and walked across the room to me. He handed me the bag and clapped me on the shoulder.

"Here's three hundred dollars," he told me. "I don't know for sure how much land that would buy in Texas— maybe seventy-five or a hundred acres. Do what you can with it." He hopped across the room on his one leg and took a seat in the chair again. "I had a buddy in my outfit during the war who was from Texas," he told me. "He said they have some hilly country in central Texas, near Austin. That sounds like what we might want. It'll remind me of Kentucky a bit. See what you can do there."

I looked at the money in my hand, grateful both for the trust they were placing in me and for the information that could narrow down my search. As he'd said, Texas was indeed a big place. I glanced up briefly, trying to decide how to say what had just crossed my mind.

Ike waved a hand impatiently. "You've got something on your mind. Out with it!"

I shifted my feet and glanced at Julia. "I've got a little money myself, but maybe not enough to buy some land right away," I began. "Maybe if it all works out for you with the land grant, I could buy these seventy-five or hundred acres from you and get myself a start down there..." my voice trailed off a little.

"Done!" Ike boomed. "See if you can get 'em close together. You're the best neighbor we've got around here."

We spent the rest of the afternoon making a few more plans. Ike insisted that I take his mule with me, along with some tools that might be useful in throwing up a cabin on any land that I might find. He led me out to the shed in back and had me take a couple shovels, saws and a sledgehammer. He threw in a rake and hammer, then surveyed the pile. He pointed at a box in the corner of the shed.

"Take that too," he told me. I pulled the box over and checked inside. It contained sticks of dynamite. I looked askance at Ike, who only shrugged. "Useful for clearin' out tree stumps and such," he said. I added the box to the pile of tools.

Ike led the way out of the shed. "Time to meet Lucifer," he told me. He led the way around the corner and pointed at a small, gray mule with a baleful eye. "Lucifer," he explained. I took a step or two closer, and Lucifer bared his teeth at me. I backed up a step and turned back around to look at Ike. "You got anything else?" I asked. Ike chuckled and pulled a carrot out of his back pocket. He held it out to me. "Give him a few o' these and he'll be your friend," he promised. I held out the carrot, and Lucifer snatched it out of my hand, glaring at me while he chewed it. "Okay," I said doubtfully, "I'll try it."

The Hawkins insisted that I stay over with them that evening before leaving, and I had to admit I didn't have a better plan. The boys, Pete and Isaac, were in high spirits during dinner. I envied the sense of adventure they had about this move, with none of the worries or concerns about how it would turn out. I took my time over the food. This was the first home-cooked meal I'd really had in quite some time, and I knew it would be the last for a while.

Julia and I found our way outside to the same bench after dinner, and I looked at her from time to time, wondering if I had been a fool for these last several years. She was a beautiful girl with dark hair and green eyes. I had assumed I didn't have enough to offer a girl like this. I knew there was no shortage of suitors that found their way to the Hawkins' door, but she had chosen none of them. I was a tall man at six feet two and one hundred ninety-five pounds. When I took hold of things, they moved—working on the farm all these years had made me strong. Handsome? Well, I didn't know about that. I had dark hair and brown eyes, but I had a couple of small scars on my face, courtesy of some hand-to-hand fighting during the war.

I suddenly knew Julia had asked me a question, and I hadn't answered. I searched my mind for the last thing she'd said. Something about staying in touch...

"I'll write as soon as I know anything," I promised. "And I'll let you know where you can reach me."

She nodded and watched the shadows lengthening across the yard. "Jake," she began, "did you ever think that maybe you and I could...have gotten together somewhere along the way?"

My jaw dropped so far, I thought it would hit my knees. Maybe I *had* been a fool all this time.

I scrambled in my mind for what to say. "I didn't think...I mean, you are a b-beautiful woman," I finally managed to say.

Her face lit up.

"I thought, well, I guess I didn't think the way I should have. A woman like you, she could have her choice of a lot of men, and I...I didn't think I had much to offer." I started to say something else, then decided to quit while I was ahead.

Julia smiled, stood up, then leaned over and brushed her lips across my cheek. "You're you, Jake, and I think you have a lot to offer a girl. Don't forget that." She turned and walked back into the cabin. I remained sitting on the bench, a foolish grin spreading across my face.

Morning found me loaded up and ready to push off early. I saddled up Sherman shortly after breakfast, and Lucifer came along willingly enough after I bribed him with a couple of carrots. The family came out to see me off, and I could see hope in their eyes. Hope for a new and better life. I was feeling the same thing. They said their goodbyes one by one and walked back to the doorway. Julia lifted up a bag of fresh-baked biscuits to me and took my right hand in both of hers.

"Don't forget what I told you last night, Jake." The same silly grin seemed to be on my face this morning.

"I'll never forget what you said," I promised, then slapped Sherman on the rump. We were on the road to Texas.

———

About a month later, I pulled Sherman to a stop and sat atop a small rise, looking over the country in front of me. I had traveled steadily through Kentucky from the northeast to the southwest, then down across the tip of Tennessee. A steamboat ride had taken me across the Mississippi River. I had stayed on the steamboat a little longer than planned, just because I was enjoying the ride and the view. The river was far wider and more powerful than I had imagined. When I disembarked, I was in Arkansas, a state I had never visited before.

I didn't make any stops I didn't have to, but I had stopped to buy some food and a couple essentials in Memphis, Tennessee and again in Little Rock, Arkansas. I kept to myself and pulled off the trails a way to bed down at night. I had offers to join a couple of other groups who seemed to be headed my way, but I figured a man traveling alone could move faster, and it didn't seem like any of us needed much protection, though I didn't doubt there could be some robbers here and there. I kept my Spencer loaded and ready.

I cut down through Arkansas and crossed over into Texas, surprised at the number of pine trees I found there, and liking the area. We had agreed that I would look for land near Austin, so I kept moving. When I reached Austin, there were too many people to suit me, and I felt sure that Julia and her family would feel the same way. Now, I would guess I had come somewhere around a thousand miles, and I thought I might be looking at home. I could see a river cutting across the land and through a town down there. I nudged Sherman forward, and after a moment, Lucifer reluctantly followed.

We stopped, and I let the animals have some water, taking my time and chewing on a piece of jerky. We swam the river, and I rode Sherman into a small dusty street, taking in the sight of a few shops on each side of the road. I saw a saloon and stopped, thinking things over. I had avoided stopping for a drink at a saloon this entire time, intent on getting where I was going. It was time, I decided, to cut my thirst and see what I could find out about the name of this town and the prospects of settling here. I guided the animals to the side of the street and hitched them both to the rail.

I pushed through the doors and walked across to the bar, which seemed fairly empty—early afternoon. I carried my Spencer like it was part of me and leaned it up against the bar. The bartender glanced at my rifle, shrugged, and came over to take my order. I tossed off the whiskey he brought me and was preparing to order another when I heard a rasping, not unfriendly voice on my left.

"Where you from, pilgrim?" I turned to see an old man standing at the bar, turning his whiskey glass in his hands, and taking in my dusty buckskin clothes and the Spencer. He looked at my waist, seemed surprised not to see a pistol there, and grinned in my direction. I guessed he was talking to me.

# CHAPTER 3

## FREDERICKSBURG

I glanced around behind me, not sure if I was the *pilgrim* or not.

"Yeah, you, pilgrim," he said when I looked back around. "Wearin' them buckskin clothes, carryin' that Spencer like you was born with it. I'm talkin' to you. Prob'ly came here straight from the hills somewhere."

I finished my whiskey, set the glass down on the bar, and ordered a beer. "Kentucky," I said finally.

He chortled. "I knowed it," he crowed triumphantly. "I come from the sticks way back in Tennessee," he said, moving toward a table and waving me toward it. "You had it written all over you. Come an' drink a beer with me," he said, sitting down and shoving a chair toward me with his foot.

"What brings you to Texas?" he asked, watching my face over his beer glass as I took a seat.

"Oh, just looking for a new place," I said evasively. He snorted and took a pull from his beer.

"Had a feud back there, did ye?" he asked. I stopped with my beer halfway to my lips and locked eyes with him across the table. He chortled again. "I told ye I come from the sticks back there," he said. "I knew your story before you walked from them doors over to the bar." He settled back into his chair and watched me.

"Well," I said eventually, "there was nothing for me back there anymore."

"Meanin' there ain't no more of them left you was feudin' with back there," he filled in.

He was so uncomfortably accurate, so I decided to change the subject. "My name's Jake," I said finally. "What's yours?"

He looked at me shrewdly, finally going along with the change of subject. "Boone," he said.

"That your last name or your first?" I asked.

"Same thing," he answered. "It's my last name, but I don't use the first name my ma gave me." He removed his hat and placed it on the table, his gray mane of hair tumbling out from underneath. He threw me a look, seeming to challenge me to ask him about his first name. I let it pass.

"Jake's my name," I repeated. "Jake McCabe."

"Pleased to meetcha, Jake," he said, then settled back to give his beer some serious attention.

"What do you do around here, Boone?" I asked after a lengthy silence had developed. He shrugged.

"Mostly whatever I want to," he said. "I help out some here around the bar sometimes, do me a little carpenter work sometimes, pretty handy with a hammer, I am. I can do a little cowboyin' if I get hungry enough, but mostly, I earn my keep around this place," he said, waving at the saloon. That reminded me—I didn't even know the name of this place, the town, that is. I asked. "Fredericksburg," he said, his eyebrows shooting up in some surprise. "You must have come straight in off the trail, pilgrim...Jake," he amended after seeing my irritation.

"I did," I nodded. "What's the name of that river out there," I asked, pointing vaguely out the door.

"Guadeloupe," he answered promptly.

I absorbed that information, cracking open a few peanuts the bartender had brought over. "You lookin' to settle here, Jake?" he asked finally, studying the thoughtful expression on my face.

"Might be," I said slowly. "I want to settle down somewhere around here. This a good town for that?" He reached across the table to help himself to a few peanuts.

"Been my home for twenty years," he said. "I think you'd like it here. You got a trade? Want a ranch? Cows are a big business lately," he added. "They drive 'em up that trail and sell 'em in Kansas. Plenty o' suitable land around here for raising cows."

"No trade," I said. "I've mostly farmed and raised a few animals." I glanced around the room. "I want to buy some land to get started. For me and a family coming from Kentucky. Maybe one hundred acres to start. Raise some crops, graze some cows." Boone stared out the door thoughtfully, throwing a peanut into his mouth from time to time.

"You can do that around here," he said. He frowned briefly, started to say something, then stopped. His gaze went to my Spencer, then dropped to my waist. His mouth opened and closed without saying anything, then he reached for his beer.

"You're good with that thing, I guess?" he asked, pointing at the rifle. I nodded. "You got a sidearm?" he asked, pointing at my waist.

"No," I admitted. "Why?"

He shrugged evasively. "Rifle's not as handy," he said finally. "Might have to shoot a snake or a varmint."

I remained silent, waiting for the unspoken thoughts. Finally, he looked around the room, then leaned forward.

"Sometimes," he said, choosing his words carefully, "sometimes there's folks that like to graze their cows on other folks' grass." He waved his hand at the Spencer, thought better of whatever he was going to say, then waved for another beer. "Folks around here defend themselves more with a side-gun," he said finally. "Spencer might work if you're pretty prompt with it."

"Well," I said eventually, "I'm kinda used to that sort of thing, where I come from."

He grinned. "I was right about that feudin', back in the hills, weren't I? Are there any of 'em left?"

"No, I admitted, "there's none of them left. I was hoping to leave that sort of thing behind, though."

He thumped his beer glass back down on the table. "'Course you were," he said. "Just wanted you to be ready for what could come yore way." He seemed to leave a few thoughts unsaid still, but I decided not to press him on it.

After a while, I pointed at the revolver on his gun belt. "What have you got there?" I asked, pointing again.

He took out the gun and placed it on the table. "Smith and Wesson," he said.

I picked it up, testing the weight, then turned and sighted down the barrel. "Like it?" I asked.

He shrugged. "It's been okay," he said. "If'n I was you though, wantin' to buy one now, I'd get the new Colt revolver. Best thing I've seen. Gonna git me one when I save up some money. Got a gun shop down the street, started sellin' 'em a few weeks back. Show you where it is if'n you want."

I tossed a coin on the table and stood up. Boone drained the last of his beer, stood, and glanced at me sideways. "I kin show you where to buy clothes like we wear around here, too, if you want." I glanced down at the buckskins. *Well, maybe*, I thought.

Boone pointed out a couple stores and left me. The gun store owner looked me over skeptically when I walked in, carrying my old Spencer. He brightened up when I told him I wanted to look at the Colt revolvers. He laid a couple models out on a table for me. One was noticeably longer than the other. He explained that one had a 4 ¾ inch barrel, and the other had a 7 ½ inch barrel. I tested the feel of both in my hand, not sure what I wanted. The man watched me for a minute.

"If you're not used to a revolver, I'd get the four and three-quarter inch barrel," he suggested. "Easier to handle, less bulky."

That made sense to me. I cringed at the price but bought the Colt and a gun belt with a holster. He glanced at the Spencer.

"I've got a new Winchester '73 rifle that can fire the same .44 caliber ammunition as the Colt," he told me.

"One thing at a time," I told him. "My pockets are light enough as it is."

I stopped at a general store to buy a few new clothes that left me looking less like a stranger from the hills, along with a pair of boots. Maybe if I looked less like a stranger, I'd be less likely to run into the kind of trouble Boone was talking about. After a stop at the livery stable to leave Lucifer until I could figure out what to do with him, I decided to treat myself to a couple nights in a boarding house. After checking in, I went out and stood outside the boarding house, thumbs hooked under my belt, looking to the west and north. There were several gently sloping hills out beyond the river. I could see a few deer feeding in the pastures. I could picture living here, running some cows and maybe planting a small crop every year.

I turned and began walking down the street, looking for a place to eat. A few people passed me by. I tipped my hat in return to a few greetings people gave me. I passed a saloon, the sounds of a piano and general hubbub spilling out to the street. I kept going, not much interested in joining them. Saloons were a good place to pick up news and information, but I wasn't in the mood right now. At length, I came to a stop underneath a sign, squinting to read it against the setting sun. "Good Eats," it announced. I shrugged and went inside. I was willing to find out how good they really were.

———

Julia stood in the cabin's door, watching her father, Ike, with a small smile on her face. Ike was pretty much known as an old horse trader, and that was exactly what he was doing now. They were going to need two horses, young and strong enough to pull a loaded wagon to Texas. They had only one, a mare about ten years old. Their other horse, referred to affectionately as *Ol' Tom* by the family, was neither young enough nor strong enough to fill the bill. He had some value remaining, and Ike was out there in the yard trying to get full value.

Ike was circling around a seven-year-old gelding in the yard, making critical comments as he went.

"Looks a little knock-kneed," he announced as he leaned forward on his crutch to peer at the gelding's knees. "You sure he hasn't been hurt pulling that plow of yours?"

Their neighbor only snorted derisively and waved a hand in the air. "Never been hurt a day in his life. Better than I can say for that old nag of yours. I need Ol' Tom plus fifty dollars cash for this horse." Ike recoiled and laid a hand over his heart, feigning genuine pain. Julia, struggling not to laugh out loud at her father's antics, turned and went back into the cabin.

She walked back to the table next to the old wood stove and resumed her efforts to can as many early vegetables from the garden as she could before it was time to go. She figured food and clothing might be the most valuable things they could bring. They had basically no furniture worth bringing, and there would be no need to weigh down the wagon with it. They had already given away several things that would have served only to weigh the wagon down.

The neighbors in and around the nearest town had reacted with surprise when they heard about the Hawkins family's plan to move. They had almost all reacted with relief when they found out that Jake had preceded them in making the move. The feud between the McCabe's and Mueller's families had grown old for all of them, and they seemed glad to be rid of it at any cost. Julia finished the canning she was doing at the moment and made bread dough for the evening meal.

She thought of Jake as a man who just hadn't found what he needed yet in life. His family was tied down to a small, poor piece of land here in Kentucky, and none of the others had been willing to try again somewhere else. Jake had honored the family by staying and doing the best he could with it, but the feud with the Mueller family had destroyed what little he had here. Julia saw him as a strong, hard-working, good man who could do well for himself with a fresh chance in a place offering more opportunity. She hoped she could be a part of that new start.

Her thoughts were interrupted by the sound of Ike hopping through the cabin door, muttering to himself. "How much is he taking you for, Dad?" she asked, teasing him.

Ike pulled open the drawer containing the cash they had left, looking pleased with himself. "Taking me for?" he demanded. "That greenhorn never saw the day he could take Ike Hawkins. I'm givin' him tired, swaybacked Ol' Tom and forty dollars for his horse. He don't even know what happened to him." He pulled the gold pieces out of the drawer and turned around.

"Whatever you say, Dad," Julia told him.

"Don't forget it," he said, heading out to the yard to complete the trade.

Dinner at the Hawkins' house followed the pattern they had settled into after Jake had left for Texas. The boys, Pete and Isaac, excited by the prospect of moving, talked at length about things they planned to do once they had moved. Ike listened to the boys and chuckled at some of the boasting, stopping now and then to talk to Julia. It was her mother Julia was worried about. She had always seemed quiet, even withdrawn, but now she seemed to keep all her thoughts to herself. Ike glanced her way from time to time, then asked Julia to join him outside for a talk after the meal.

They seated themselves on the bench outside, and Ike launched into his thoughts without preamble.

"The way I see it," he said, "you're going to have to be the backbone of this family when we get to Texas."

"That's you, Dad," she protested immediately. "It has always been you."

Ike patted her hand and leaned back on the bench. "I'll be there for all of us—always have been and always will be." He nodded. "But I don't get around like I used to,"—here he pointed at his leg—"and I'm not getting any younger." He cut off her response in mid-sentence. "The boys are getting big enough and strong enough to do the hard work, but they'll need some direction. It can't all come from me, and I won't be around forever. They need you to guide them, too."

Julia settled back to hear the rest of it, sensing he wasn't done. "I'm worried about your mother," he said shortly. "She's never been strong, the way you're strong, and deep down, I don't think she wants this move." He stared out into the trees absently. "She won't come out and say that, but she doesn't want to pull up stakes and move. I have to do it for the three of you. There's no real future for us here. The land isn't that rich, and there's just not enough of it. You and the boys need a place where you can really do something for yourselves. I think Texas might just be that place."

They lapsed into silence for a while. Julia decided to air the concerns that troubled her the most about the move. "What if we run into real trouble?" she asked.

Ike turned to look at her. "What do you mean by *real trouble*?"

Julia motioned toward the old McCabe land. "I mean something like what happened to the McCabes around here. Trouble with neighbors, maybe shooting trouble. Somebody that wants to push us off our land. Could we hold it if we have to? We don't know anybody down there."

"Hmmm...you do think things through, don't you?" Ike smiled at her approvingly. "That's why you'll be the rock of this family. Well," he said at length, "I can still stand my ground and shoot if I need to. The boys are getting bigger and stronger all the time." He looked down at his hands thoughtfully. "And, you're wrong, you know. We do know somebody down there. Jake would stand with us. He's somebody to be reckoned with if something like this comes along."

Julia nodded her head several times. "Yes, he is. And I'm sure he would stand with us if something bad came along."

Ike patted her hand and moved to stand up. "You know," he said, "I'll bet you could really make him a part of this family if you set your mind to it."

Julia felt a blush creeping across her face. She opened her mouth to say something, thought better of it, and gave Ike a playful slap on the arm. He chuckled and swung back into the cabin.

# CHAPTER 4

## BUILDING A HOME

"You done went and bought some new clothes. Now I can't call you Pilgrim no more." I looked up from my breakfast to see Boone looking down at me. I motioned with my hand for him to take a seat across the table, but he was already seated, waving at the waiter for some coffee. I glanced down at my fresh shirt and denim pants. I had to admit they were pretty comfortable. "You ain't wearin' a sidearm yet, I see," he announced, slurping down his coffee while he spoke.

I shook my head. "I bought one," I admitted, "just wasn't comfortable wearing it yet. Maybe I'll take it out and practice with it for a while first."

"Good idea." He nodded. He wagged his forefinger in the air. "One word of advice. Take your time and hit what you're aimin' at."

I nodded my head in agreement. My dad had told me something similar when he gave me the old Spencer. It was excellent advice.

"What's next for ye, Jake? You said somethin' about buying some land, right?"

I chewed my food absently, wondering how he seemed to know what I was thinking. "That's what I'm up to today," I agreed. "I plan to go over there," I said, pointing toward the bank across the street, "and see what I can find out."

"You could do that," said Boone, "or you can come with me an' I'll show you one of the best pieces o' property around. Prob'ly get it pretty cheap, too." He grabbed a piece of bread that had been served with the coffee and downed it in two bites.

I tilted my head back and watched his face, trying to figure out if he was serious. He appeared to be. "How do you know so much about it?" I asked.

He shrugged. "Ol' Boone here works in the saloon and keeps his ears open an' his mouth shut."

Well, I had my doubts about how much he kept his mouth shut, but the saloon was a pretty good place to learn things about a town. "Okay," I said, "I'll bite. Tell me about this property."

He talked around his mouthful of bread and pointed at my plate. "Finish up. I'll take you to it as soon as you're done."

Finding myself suddenly eager to see the property, I wolfed down the rest of my breakfast, and we took a quick fifteen-minute ride into the gentle hills to the west of Fredericksburg. On the way, I reined in for a moment and pointed toward a pink, rocky dome rising up to the north of us.

"What's that?" I asked.

Boone swung around and looked at what I was indicating. "Oh, that," he said, leaning over in the saddle to spit. "Called Enchanted Rock. Folks say it's romantic. Take picnics up there an' such." He turned and led the way to the west again.

I chuckled at how unimpressed he was with it, but made a mental note about the picnics.

He left the main trail rather suddenly to follow a narrow, twisting path through a stand of live oak and black cherry trees. We emerged from the trees onto a wide, flat bench. As we crossed the bench, I could see that it gave way and sloped down gently to a large meadow, ringed by trees on both sides. It curved off into the distance in front of us. I could see cattle grazing some distance away. I pulled up, impressed by what I saw. It appeared to be a rich, green valley dotted by an occasional clump of wildflowers. The wildflowers were slowly giving way to the heat of late spring. A creek cut across the lower one-third of the pasture and formed a pond at one end.

Boone looked over my way and grinned. "Purty, ain't it? I bet you can get it cheap, too."

The last statement jarred me. I took another quick look around me. "What's wrong with it? Why would it be cheap?"

Boone took his time answering me, finally pointing off into the distance. "See those cows down there?"

I nodded.

"Well...those cows are owned by a big rancher named Diehl...Virgil Diehl. You could say he has a habit of grazin' his cows on property he don't own. When folks take exception to it, he leans on 'em pretty hard. Not too many folks really want to be his neighbors."

I took a minute to digest that one. "He ran the last owner off?" I asked.

Boone nodded. "You could say that."

I took a minute to look around the land. I had to

remember I was buying this for the Hawkins family...and maybe myself if they sold it to me after they got their grant. I thought about old Ike Hawkins, then about Julia. Would they want to get into a situation like this? I looked again at the beauty and the promise of this land. I was betting they would be willing to take a chance on it. I looked back over at Boone. "So," I said, "this Diehl is a bully."

Boone nodded and spat. "You could say that. He mostly pays others to do his bullying for him, but yeah, he's a bully."

"Well," I intoned, "most bullies just need a good punch in the nose."

His laugh rang out so loud and so suddenly that Sherman sidestepped a couple times on me. Boone leaned over the saddle and really let himself go. "Pilgrim," he said, "I like the way you're lookin' at this. I might even buy me a ticket for this one." He chortled a few more times, then looked over at me. "Seriously," he said, "if'n you need somebody to watch yore back on this one, you can count on me. I don't like bullies no more'n you do." He reached his hand out over the saddle, and we shook on it.

————

I sat across the desk from a man at the Fredericksburg State Bank. The name I saw on a plaque on his desk announced that he was Mark Hayes, president of the bank. He got me a cup of coffee and got down to business. "So," he said, "it sounds like you're interested in buying the old Richardson property." I had explained where the land was located, and apparently, the former

owners were named Richardson. The bank had fore-
closed and reclaimed the property after the Richardsons
had left town.

"I am," I said, "but I won't be buying it for me. I'm
buying it in the name of Ike and Jeanne Hawkins." Hayes
looked at me quizzically. "They're moving here pretty
soon. From Kentucky. I'll watch it for them until then."

Hayes sat back and nodded. "Okay, Mr. McCabe," he
said. "It's one hundred-thirty acres. Prime country. It
would normally cost about $250, but I'll sell it to you for
$200. How do you—how do the Hawkins—plan to pay
for this?"

I reached into a side pocket inside my jacket and
pulled out a small burlap bag. I counted out $200 and
pushed it across the desk. "Cash money," I said.

Hayes's eyebrows lifted, and he counted the coins. A
smile crossed his face. "This won't take but a few minutes
to fill out some papers. Make yourself comfortable, Mr.
McCabe."

Fifteen minutes later, I stood outside the bank with
the papers for the land tucked into my jacket. I had
asked Hayes about the veteran grant program. He said he
knew little about it—I might have to go to the Austin
area to talk to a government man about it. Hayes said he
thought there was land in the area that could be put in a
grant. I decided it was time to visit the saloon and
crossed the street for a quick celebration. After a couple
of cold beers, I went to the general store and bought
myself some paper and a pencil. I carried them out to
the main street and found a bench, then sat down to
write a letter to Julia. I struggled to get started, then
finally just decided to tell her the news I had for the
family.

*Dear Julia,*

*I hope you and the family are still doing well. By now, I guess you're just about ready to come to Texas. I reached a place here just a little west of Austin and bought some land. The name of the town is Fredericksburg, and it lies close to the Guadeloupe River. There are hills and pretty country all around. I hope it will remind you of Kentucky.*

*I bought 130 acres of land for $200 earlier this morning. I'm planning to start building a cabin on it with the money I have left from what Ike gave me. I met someone here who does some building and I think he will help me. I hope to have a place for you to move into when you get here.*

*If you write me, you can just send the letter to the post office in Fredericksburg. I'll ask them to hold any letters I get at the post office for me to pick up.*

*I'll see what else I can find out about the grant program. I hope you'll be starting on your way soon now. I can't wait to see you.*

*Yours,*
*Jake.*

I read the letter over about four times and finally decided I wasn't ever going to get completely happy with it, so I just took it over and mailed it.

———

I had no idea about building a cabin, but Boone had said he did some building, besides his saloon work. I found him in the saloon that evening, mopping floors and sorting out some boxes in the back room. I offered to buy him a beer when he took a break. He put down the mop as soon as I offered, walked over to a table, and took a seat. I glanced over at the owner behind the bar who just shrugged and went back to work.

"He lets you take a break anytime, huh?" I asked, taking another look over at the bar.

The owner had gone on with what he was doing, taking no notice of Boone.

Boone hoisted his beer and took a long pull. "He lets me sleep in the back room, an' I just do some cleaning up and carrying boxes and such. As long as I do enough to make him happy, he don't really care about my schedule." The beer glass came back down with a thump. "What's on your mind?"

"Cabin," I said shortly. "I need to build a cabin for this family so they have a place when they get here."

Boone squinted off into the distance. "How big? How many of 'em? Permanent or temporary?"

"Five of them," I said. "Temporary. I don't know, maybe fifty feet by thirty feet. They'll need a place where the stovepipe can go through the roof."

Boone looked at me shrewdly. "You do a lot for these people, Pilgrim," he observed. He took another look at me. "How old is their daughter?"

I was halfway through a sip of beer and spluttered a little, putting the glass back down. "I said nothing about a daughter," I said evasively.

Boone chortled. "You didn't have to. I can read you like a book. C'mon, how old? She purty?"

"Twenty-five, I think. Yes, she's pretty. Can we go back to the cabin building?" Boone finished his beer, vastly pleased with himself.

When he saw he wasn't getting anything else out of me about Julia, Boone settled back down to business. "Log cabin, that's easy and pretty quick. They bring lumber and logs up the river from Victoria on steamboats, sometimes. You can get the logs that way. They'll offload in Fredericksburg if'n you'll meet 'em, prob'ly. You need to get a wagon at the livery stable to haul 'em out to where you'll build. Pick the highest spot on that plateau so water'll run away from the cabin. You'll need some flat boards for the roof, an' a couple of axes for notching the logs." Everything made sense for me except the last part about two axes.

"I have an axe," I said. "Why do I need two?"

"I don't have one. You want me to hep you, don't ya?"

I nodded gratefully. "I have about seventy-five dollars left for the logs, but I..."

"You can prob'ly get what you need for that," he said. "You don't need to pay me." He waved away my protests with one hand. "Buy me a beer once in a while. Have me over for supper now an' then when you get set up over there. I have what I need and I do what I want." The subject seemed to be closed, so I bought him one more beer, then watched him go back to work.

———

Boone advised me how to put in an order for the logs and boards I would need. They told me it would take about two weeks for things to arrive, so I spent the time putting up a makeshift corral for Sherman and Lucifer on the land. There were plenty of trees surrounding the property, so I scoured the area for fallen branches and tree trunks, using Sherman to haul them back to the plateau at the top of the property. I dug holes and sank some bigger tree trunks for posts, then nailed branches across between them. It wasn't the prettiest corral, but it worked. I could quit paying the livery stable to keep Lucifer. The Hawkins could have him back when they arrived.

When the logs arrived, work went faster than I'd expected. Boone came out most days, and we notched the logs and placed them on top of each other, making a rectangular cabin on the high point of the plateau. We sank a log in the middle of the cabin and used it as a support for a long log across the top. Then we nailed the boards in for a sloping, A-shaped roof. We cut a hole in the top to ventilate the stove. We were done in a couple weeks, and I took pride when we were done. It would serve as a temporary cabin for Julia and her family.

---

Celebration of the completed cabin took place at the saloon, and of course, I was buying, since Boone had supplied most of the knowledge and a lot of the labor involved. I had received a letter from Julia that day, letting me know they would be leaving soon. Actually, considering the time it had probably taken the letter to get here, they were probably on their way now. I was leaning back and enjoying how things were turning out when Boone changed the mood. He leaned forward, grabbed my arm, and motioned with his head.

"That's him," he said.

I glanced in the direction he had shown me. "Who?"

"Virgil Diehl," he said.

I looked over again and saw a man a little older than

me, shorter than me and a little on the stocky side, dressed very well, with a gun on his hip. The gun didn't surprise me, as I was wearing one myself these days. Behind him, though, were two other men. One was a big man—my height but probably twenty pounds heavier, and none of it looked like fat. The other was considerably smaller, wearing double tied-down guns. Diehl looked around for a while, his gaze finally settling on Boone and me. He began walking toward our table.

"Big guy is called Bull—don't know his real name," Boone told me in an undertone. "He's a brawler. The smaller guy with the guns is named Karras. He fancies himself a gunfighter, as you can prob'ly tell."

Diehl walked up to the table and tipped his hat. "Boone," he said. He looked at me and extended his hand. "Diehl," he said. "Virgil Diehl."

I shook his hand without rising from the table. "Jake McCabe." I didn't offer him a seat.

Diehl looked at me uncertainly for a moment. He smiled, but the smile didn't reach his eyes. "I hear you bought the old Richardson place," he offered.

I nodded.

"Well, that makes us neighbors," he said. "I own the place north of there."

I gestured at Boone. "That's what Boone tells me." Diehl glanced at Boone and the smile faded from his mouth.

"I think," he said rather loudly, "that neighbors should be friendly. The Richardsons let me graze my cows over there sometimes. That's a good thing for a neighbor to do, don't you think?" I looked him over for a minute, then finished my beer.

"Well," I said, "that depends."

"Depends on what?" he asked.

"Well," I continued, "if the neighbor isn't grazing any cows himself and gets paid something for the use of his land, sure. Of course, if the neighbor has some cows himself, then every man's cows need to graze his own grass."

Diehl's eyes narrowed, and Bull took a few steps in my direction. I noticed the saloon got awfully quiet very quickly. As Bull got closer, I pushed back my chair and stood up. Then we all heard the unmistakable sound of a shotgun being cocked. Nance, the saloon owner, laid the shotgun across the bar.

"Virgil," he said, "I told you last time if anybody starts bustin' up this saloon with another fight, he gets shot this time. I mean it."

Diehl turned, checked the look in Nance's eye, and began walking to the door. "C'mon Bull," he said. "Another time."

Bull gave me a look and followed Diehl out the door. Karras, the guy with double guns, followed Bull.

The saloon noise started back up as I took my seat. Nance put the shotgun back under the bar. Boone slowly eased his hand away from his gun belt and waved at Nance for another beer.

"I'm buyin' this time, Pilgrim. You done started it now. This could get interestin'."

# CHAPTER 5

# CROSSING THE MISSISSIPPI

J ulia stood in the farmyard and looked at the meager possessions her family had to begin their journey west. They had a wagon, loaded only with their clothes and some tools and canned goods. They had no space in the wagon for furniture, nor could the horses pull the weight. The family had only four horses altogether, despite Ike's best trading and dealing. We hitched two horses to the wagon, which would carry both her parents plus one of her brothers in the back. Julia and her brother Pete, the older of the two boys, would ride horseback alongside the wagon. Pete had spent the last two years saving enough money for his own horse. The mule had gone to Texas already with Jake, and they had sold the old milk cow, judging the animal to be too old to make the trip.

They'd had very little sendoff from the little town where they had lived all their lives. A few families had dropped by with small gifts, but they hadn't stayed to visit at all, despite urging from Ike. Julia suspected they were glad to be rid of any connection to the McCabe-Mueller feud, no matter how slight that connection might be. Their support of the Confederacy united the town, and most of the county during the war. That put almost everyone at odds with the McCabes, and Julia's family was known to be friends with the McCabe family. The feud had been unpleasant for all of them, and Julia couldn't blame them for wanting to put it behind them. She made one last sweep through the cabin and found nothing they had left behind. She came back out and mounted her horse. Ike clucked to urge the horses forward, and they began their trip to Texas with no one to see them off.

———

Four uneventful weeks later, they found themselves at the banks of the Mississippi River. Julia and Ike walked along the storefronts and shops near Memphis, and determined pretty quickly that they wouldn't be booking passage on one of the steamboats working up and down the river. They would have to use one of the ferries crossing the river to take their wagon and horses across. A conversation with one agent convinced them it would work best to find another family or a few other travelers to share passage with them.

Leaving her mother and brothers to watch the horses and the few farm implements from the back of the wagon, Ike and Julia drove the wagon up and down the road leading to the Mississippi dock, looking for somebody they might team up with to cross the river. Seeing a small family standing beside a wagon similar to their own, Ike pulled his wagon over and waved at the family.

A tall, narrow-shouldered man detached himself from the group and moved over to them.

"Looking to cross over on a ferry?" Ike asked as the man approached them.

He nodded hesitantly. "I guess it'll be a ferry, all right," he drawled, keeping a few paces back from them.

Ike nodded. "That's what we're thinkin'," Ike said, gesturing back behind them on the road. "My wife, my two boys, and my daughter Julia here," he said, now waving his hand toward Julia. "We got to cross, an' we'd like to split the cost with somebody like us."

The man brightened a little and took a couple steps toward them. "Me, my wife, an' two little girls need to cross," he drawled. "Can't afford no steamboat, we can't. I guess it's a ferry. Heard bad things about the boilers on them ferries, though."

Ike and Julia exchanged puzzled glances. "Boilers?" Ike leaned forward.

The man nodded. "Heard tell they blow up time to time, that's what we heard...got to get across the river some way, though. Got to get to my brother's place near Austin."

"First I've heard about the boilers," Ike said slowly. "Don't they all have boilers, though? Steamboats, ferries, barges?"

The man nodded his agreement. "That's true," he acknowledged. "Like I said, we got to get across some way." He glanced at the wagon. "You got to get anything across besides that wagon and them horses?"

"Two more horses, my wife and two boys," Ike said. "I reckon we could all fit on a small ferry, pretty cheap."

The man considered things for a moment, then held

out his hand. "Jackson," he said, "Luke Jackson. My wife over there is Irene."

Ike shook his hand. "Ike," he said, "Julia. My wife is Jeanne. Let's cross that river."

The man smiled briefly, then turned to walk back to his family. They talked briefly, then he loaded his little girls into the wagon and they all moved down to join up with Ike and Julia. With the two families herded together near the dock, Ike and Luke moved off to talk to some ferry boat owners.

Ike moved along a path that followed the shore, making a distinctive sight as he leaned on his crutch, Luke Jackson following along behind, looking over the ferries as he passed them.

"Need passage across, cap'n?"

Ike turned to see who was speaking. A hawk-nosed man, skin burned by the sun, eyed them inquisitively.

"This your boat?" Ike asked, looking it over from both sides.

"Aye, cap'n, it's mine."

Ike turned back and looked him over. "How many crossings have you made?" he asked.

The man shrugged. "Lost count a long time ago, cap'n. I guarantee you I know every sandbar and hazard out there, if that's what you're worried about."

"How old is your ferry?" Luke spoke for the first time.

The man looked at the ship, thinking. "I'd say fifteen year or so. I bought 'er about seven year ago. She's good and seaworthy, she is."

Luke nodded briefly. "What about the engine? Boiler. You git those checked lately?"

The man waved impatiently. "Sure, sure." He looked at them curiously. "Just the two of you?"

Ike shook his head. "Two families, two wagons, several horses. Six horses. You take that many?"

The sailor nodded his head. "Sure."

They haggled about the price for several minutes and finally struck a bargain on the passage.

———

It surprised Julia to find out that the crossing would take them less than an hour, even though the barge had to do some maneuvering to avoid sandbars and other dangers in the river. The bargeman had told her that the river was about a mile across at this site. She had stayed with the horses for several minutes to help soothe them when the barge set out with considerable noise. Smoke poured out, both from the stack above the ship and seemingly from behind it as well. Julia wondered how much smoke there was supposed to be. After a while, things had settled down, and the horses had calmed.

She stood at the bow, watching the muddy waters curve away as the barge plowed through. She cast a wary eye backward from time to time, unnerved by Luke's mention of boiler explosions in several boats. After a while, Luke's wife, Irene, came forward and introduced herself. It seemed that the Jackson's background was not unlike her own. They came from a small, poor farm in Tennessee and were headed toward some land owned by Luke's brother. They were hopeful of improving their lot in life on the more abundant land available in Texas.

Farther back, on the railing at the port side of the barge, Ike and Luke were engaged in a discussion about the rest of their prospective trips. Luke made a proposal that they join forces for the trip as far as Austin. Ike gazed into the muddy water of the river, wondering whether such a move would slow them down. "It would make things safer for both of us," Luke said, pressing his point. "I know I have more need than you do—I have the two little girls, an' you have your two big boys plus your grown daughter. But I can take a turn watching at night." Ike turned to look at him. "Watching for what?"

"Horse thieves," came the instant reply. "People get robbed on these trails. You better be watchin' your stock at night, whether or not you're with us."

Ike turned that one over in his mind, and it made sense. Texas was no doubt a more wide-open place than they had traveled through so far, and there was strength in numbers. It was most important to get where they were going a few weeks later with everything intact. He nodded his agreement to Luke, and they shook hands, agreeing that they would go their separate ways when they reached Austin.

Julia saw them shake hands and wondered what it was about. Her greater concern, though, was about the ferry. There was more smoke pouring out the back than when they had started, she was sure, and the engine was laboring more loudly. She was comforted by seeing the shore growing closer, but there was still a way to go. She called to the captain when she caught sight of him on deck. He stopped and waited impatiently.

"Does the boat need to slow down?" she called out. He stared at her, shook his head, and continued on. "I think there's more noise and smoke than when we started," she said as he walked away. He wheeled and stared at her, the anger was clear on his face. "Lady, this boat is fine. It always works a little harder at the end of the trip. Relax." He started to walk away, then wheeled back. "I'll thank you not to shout about the boat being in danger." He walked away, muttering something under his breath about women and tenderfeet.

The last ten minutes, as the ferry docked and finally cut power, seemed to Julia to last for more than an hour. The engine belched smoke and stopped as the family rolled the wagon off the ferry and assembled on the Arkansas shore. Ike gathered the family around and explained that they would travel with the Jackson family as far as Austin. It sounded like a good plan to her, and she was sure she could help with the little girls along the route.

They formed up a line, moving out from the dock. Ike led off with the wagon, and the others fell in line behind. Julia turned on her horse to take one more look at the river and the ferry they had crossed on. The ferry had filled in a hurry and was returning with a full load—a few passengers had shoved others aside in their hurry to cross. The ferry was now several hundred yards away and gathering speed. Then, to Julia's horror and astonishment, there was a loud explosion followed by a spout of orange flame climbing into the sky. The ferry rapidly sank.

There were screams and shouts from the people still lining the shore, seeking to cross. Here and there in the muddy river, Julia could make out the form of a passenger swimming for the shore. A barge on the shore backed up into the water, turned around and steamed into the river for a short way, picking up survivors here and there. Julia watched in horror, along with both families, as the drama played out. Within half an hour, it was clear that only a handful of passengers had been saved.

The rest had drowned, and the ferry that brought her family over had sunk.

———

I was working alongside Boone in the midday sun, filling in the small spaces between the logs where they fit together on the cabin. We had found that the mud at the edges of our pond down below contained a good amount of clay, so we thought we'd use that to make the cabin a little more airtight. I worked my way along until I reached the end of one side of the cabin and paused to swipe the sweat away from my eyes. I gazed out over the pastureland below, then wiped the sweat away again and took another look.

"Boone!"

He came from the other side of the cabin and looked at me quizzically.

"Take a look." I nodded toward the valley below.

He looked, muttered beneath his breath, then looked again. Two cowboys were pushing a herd into our pasture. There was no doubt they were coming from Diehl's land. Nobody else bordered our property.

"What do you wanna do?" Boone asked.

I wiped the clay from my hands with a wet rag and tossed the rag over to Boone. "What say we have a nice little chat with them?"

Boone grinned, wiped his hands and followed me over to the horses.

I laid my Spencer across the saddle and led the way down to the tree line and back under the cover of the trees on the east side of the pasture. Boone did likewise, and we eased our way toward the herd, not showing ourselves to the two men pushing the cows forward. When the front of the herd was close to our position, I picked up the Spencer and motioned at Boone to take a spot at the edge of the trees. He did so quietly.

"You ready?" I asked.

"Whenever you are, cap'n." I wondered how many nicknames he was going to come up with for me. I nudged Sherman out of the trees and into the pasture.

The two cowhands, who I suspected doubled as gunhands, looked up in surprise as the cattle stopped and milled. When they finally looked in my direction, the Spencer was aimed directly between them. "You boys are pushing your cows onto my land," I said.

The smaller of the two, I could see, was the one from the saloon who fancied himself a gunman.

"No, we're not," he said flatly.

I glanced his direction. "Now," I said reasonably, "you know that's not true."

"You callin' me a liar?"

He reminded me a little of a banty rooster. I shifted the Spencer, so the barrel was aimed squarely at his chest.

"I didn't call you anything," I pointed out. "I said you're well aware you're on my land with those cows."

The two exchanged glances, and one began moving away from the other, trying to flank me. "There's only one of you and two of us," he said. Boone's voice sounded from the woods. "Check your math, Junior."

I kept the Spencer aimed where it was with one hand, waved my hat in the air with the other hand and began driving the cows back toward them. They moved backward, then finally turned and began drifting back to the Diehl property with the herd.

Boone eased his horse out of the woods, then rode over to sit beside me as the Diehl cowboys and herd left the property. He glanced at the Colt I now wore every day on my hip. "You practice any with that thing?"

I nodded. "Every day I go out to the woods and practice with it."

"Good," he said. "Just take enough time to hit what you're aiming at. That's the main thing." We waited until we were sure they weren't coming back, then Boone glanced overhead at the sun, sinking lower in the west. "Whaddya say we grab some dinner at the diner, then drain a couple beers at the saloon?"

Dusk was settling in by the time we reached the saloon. Boone and I drank in relative quiet, feeling satisfaction with the progress on the cabin. The doors pushed open, and a man came through with a badge on his chest. He proceeded to our table.

"I'm Daniels," he said, looking me over with dark, rather cruel eyes. "Chase Daniels."

I stood, took his hand, and introduced myself. He nodded curtly, turned to go, then turned back.

"I want no trouble in this town," he said, giving me a challenging look.

"I don't want any trouble either," I said.

"Not what I hear," he said over his shoulder as he walked away.

I sat down and looked at Boone in some confusion. "Diehl's man," Boone said. "Everybody knows Diehl's payin' him. We need to get him voted out."

The doors opened again, and Diehl came in with Bull. They looked around till they spotted me, then walked over to the bar. Chatter resumed in the saloon, and I thought maybe we would still have a peaceful evening. I walked over to the bar to order a refill. Bull saw me coming in the mirror, turned, stepped away from the bar, then gave me a deliberate shove on the way by.

It was a classic setup for a fight. I stumbled, regained my balance, then turned to go to the bar. Bull was standing to the side, fists up. "You pushed me!" I took one look and knew there was no backing down from him. "No," I said. "You either pushed me, or you're drunk, or else you're just plain clumsy." His lips parted in a fierce grin and he started toward me.

The sound of a shotgun cocking interrupted us. The barkeep laid the shotgun over the bar. "Bull," he said, "you take this outside or else I'll take you outside in a coffin." Bull looked at me, then the shotgun, then turned and started toward the door. "Outside," he told me. "Unless you're just plain yellow."

He went through the batwing doors, and Boone eased up beside me. "He's a dirty fighter," he said. "He'll throw dirt in your eyes, anything else he can think of. You do much fightin'?"

"Lots," I said. "We boys grew up fighting all the time. Plus, I had a guy in my unit in the army, knew a lot about boxing. He taught me some things I can use against this guy." Boone's eyes brightened. "Prizefightin', you mean?"

"Right," I said. Boone reached out to hold my hat. He stared out the saloon window. "You think you can take this guy?"

"I think so," I told him.

"After you," Boone said. "This could be fun."

# CHAPTER 6

## HORSE THIEVES

The crowd spilled out of the saloon behind me and pretty quickly formed a circle around the two of us. I saw some money exchanging hands here and there. Bull made quite a spectacle of taking off his shirt, spitting into his hands and circling around. At the edge of the crowd, I saw the sheriff. He seemed to be content staying at the back of the crowd. I returned my attention to Bull, who advanced to the center of the little circle that surrounded us. He was smiling at the crowd, stopping to motion at me, telling me he was going to destroy me.

I walked slowly to meet him at the center of the oval, noticing that he held his left hand low and his right hand higher. I guessed that he ended a lot of fights pretty fast by loading up that big overhand right. I circled him, moving in and out. I leaned back, letting that big right hand swing by harmlessly, then stepped in and hit him twice with my left, striking him sharply on the right eye. He blinked in surprise and tried the same thing again. I dodged his swing again, then stepped and hit him twice more above the right eye, jolting his head back sharply with each punch. His right eye swelled, and a trickle of blood came down his cheek.

He circled me warily now, not quite so sure what to do when he failed to connect with that right hand. I faked another punch with my left, and he leaned away. I swung a hard right cross over that left hand he held so low, and he stumbled backward from the force of it, letting out a yell of surprise and rage. He set himself and rushed me, arms outstretched, trying to wrap me up and drive me down to the ground. I took a step back and went down, putting my right foot under his belly as I went on my back. I shoved upward with my right leg and launched him into the crowd behind me.

He disentangled himself from the crowd and came at me in a low lunge. His left hand came up, and he threw a handful of dirt into my eyes. Momentarily blinded, I staggered backward. He caught me with a hard, looping punch, and I covered up and ducked instinctively. The punches that would have finished me off went harmlessly overhead. I circled and dodged a couple more punches, shaking my head to clear my vision. He crowded me, throwing one punch after another. None landed solidly, and I managed to back him off with two more left-handed punches to the face. His right eye was swollen almost shut now.

We circled a few more times, and I heard the crowd get onto him. I doubted that any of his fights had lasted this long before. I saw anger and impatience building on his face, and he charged in, trying to finish with that hard right. I faked another punch with my left hand, and he lifted one hand to block, leaning away toward my right to avoid another punishing blow. I swung a hard, straight overhand right and broke his nose.

He staggered past me and fell to his knees, bleeding into the dust and breathing raggedly. He swung around, still on his knees, and this time, I saw him scooping up dirt with his right hand. He came off the ground with a bellow and charged me, flinging the dust toward my face. I closed my eyes and dodged to my right. As he charged past me, slightly off-balance, I set my feet and clasped my hands together. Then I swung both hands like a club, connecting with the side of his head as he went past. It sounded like the butt end of an axe striking a log. He fell to the dust, face down. He was out cold.

I stood where I was, wiping my eyes with my sleeve, still feeling the sting of the dirt he'd thrown at me. I touched my left eye gently where he'd connected with that one hard punch. I winced, then turned when I heard the sheriff's voice. "McCabe, I told you I wanted a quiet, clean town. Brawlers get to stay in my jail." He came from the other side of the street, hand hovering over his pistol.

Nance, the saloon owner, stepped between us. "Fair fight, sheriff," he exclaimed. "Bull started it. I know. It was in my saloon." The general store owner stepped out from the crowd and stood beside Nance. "True, sheriff," he said. "I was in there and saw it. You arresting people now for defending themselves?" The local baker, somebody I'd never even met, joined the other two and stood in front of me. "If you're arresting innocent people for stopping a brawler like Bull, I guess I'll need to talk to some people about that election in a few weeks," he said. I sensed movement, and a few others gathered behind me. Daniels, the sheriff, stopped and looked at the three of them, a scowl growing on his face. Finally, muttering under his breath, he turned and walked away.

I started to thank them for stepping in for me, but they waved me off. "We just told the truth," Nance said. "That's a crooked sheriff, and we plan to send him on his way, but we'll do it legal. All we need is a good man to take his place, and this town will vote him out. Diehl's had his way long enough." He stopped and watched me stroking my bruised knuckles. "Come on back in the saloon," he said. "I'll get you some ice for that."

I watched as Bull lurched slowly to his feet. Diehl, his face a giant thundercloud, helped Bull get over to his horse and into the saddle. He glared at me as they rode away. Boone was clearly in some high spirits as I turned toward the saloon. "Eighty dollars!" he chortled. "Eighty dollars I made!" I stared at him. "You bet on me to win that fight?"

"Sure, I did" he crowed. "I'd have bet your money too if'n you'd let me hold it. You said punch a bully in the nose, but I didn't think you'd do it literal. Dang! Old Bull gonna be breathin' sideways for a while." He extended twenty bucks toward me. "Here," he said, "you earned this. Plus, I'll buy you a beer." He held one of the batwing doors open for me and clapped me on the shoulder as I re-entered the saloon.

I glanced back over my shoulder as I entered. Diehl and Bull were riding away, Diehl steadying Bull with one hand as they went. I knew this wasn't over.

———

They wound through East Texas, getting closer to the goal day by day. They took turns watching the horses at night, and so far, nobody had come near the horses or caused trouble. Julia would take her first shift that night, being relieved by Ike in the wee hours of the morning. Ike had splurged with some of the remaining money he had, buying a new Winchester '73 for Julia and each of the boys. It was, he said, the kind of thing they could use in Texas to shoot deer and varmints. She wasn't quite sure what he meant by varmints, but she had practiced with it quite a bit before they left. She wasn't too sure Ike even knew what varmints they had in Texas.

She was surprised by her introduction to Texas— there were tall, thick stands of pine trees everywhere. They went by a lake that looked like what she would have expected of a Louisiana bayou. And the humidity was thick. She hoped that central Texas wouldn't be as humid. Her other concern was her mother, Jeanne, who had become even more quiet and withdrawn on this trip, if that were possible. It worried Julia that maybe Jeanne was sick and not telling anyone about it.

She urged her horse up alongside the wagon, coming up on Ike's side. Ike had done almost all the driving of the cart so far. Yesterday, he had finally relented and let Pete drive for a couple of hours, after Julia had pointed out that the boy needed to learn how. If Jeanne was quieter and more withdrawn since leaving on the trip, her father was the exact opposite. Ike grew more excited and verbal as they went. Hearing Julia's horse coming alongside, Ike turned his head, broke into a broad grin and gestured at the countryside with one hand.

"Look at all this land, daughter of mine!" he shouted excitedly. "There will be lots of land for you and your brothers. Lots of land to call your own and raise your family on. I *love* this place," he shouted.

Julia couldn't help but laugh at her dad for about the tenth time since they had crossed into Texas. Her father's excitement was absolutely infectious.

Julia glanced over at her mother, and Ike took notice.

"I think yer mom don't feel so good," he said, lowering his voice considerably. "I wanted her to ride in the wagon back there today, but she wouldn't go. She says she feels fine, but I don't believe her. Maybe you can talk to her after we stop tonight."

Julia looked at Jeanne again and nodded her head in agreement, then she dropped back again to follow the wagon. Jeanne looked flushed. Julia was guessing she had a fever.

After the group set up camp and had supper that evening, she noticed that Jeanne moved away from the group and sat on a rock near the campfire. Julia picked up a blanket, walked over, and offered her the blanket. Jeanne accepted it in silence and wrapped it around herself loosely. After a long silence, Julia finally turned to face her mother.

"Mom, do you feel okay?"

Jeanne only shrugged. Julia reached out with the back of her hand to touch her mother's cheek. *It felt hot*, she thought.

"Do you want to lie down in the back of the wagon for a couple days?"

No response.

"Do we need to stop for a few days to rest?"

Finally, Jeanne gathered herself and turned to face her. "I don't want to stop," she said firmly. "I want to get there."

After several more minutes had passed without

conversation, Julia rose, went to the wagon to get her Winchester, and moved off to take the first watch.

Heavy clouds overhead had considerably dimmed the glow from the full moon, making her night watch job a little more difficult tonight. Julia picked a spot near the horses underneath a large pine tree. She brushed together a pile of fallen pine needles to soften her position and leaned back against the tree trunk, confident she wouldn't be visible for more than a few yards in her dark clothing. Her thoughts turned to her future and what needed to be done when they arrived at the land Jake had bought for them.

So much depended on the land grant. With 1,280 acres, they could eventually build a herd of cattle and do some farming for a good living from the land, she was sure. Without the grant, the 130 acres Jake had bought for them wouldn't provide for them nearly as well, but they could all do what they had done in Kentucky. The boys had looked after the small amount of livestock they had owned. Julia had taught school, her mother had taken in some sewing, and Ike had a small blacksmithing business. They had been able to bring only a few of the smaller tools and had sold the anvil and bigger, heavier items.

She wondered again, as she had throughout this trip, where Jake fit into the plans. If they were able to get the grant, would he help them run and manage the ranch? Ike wouldn't be able to get around well enough to do it, and the boys would need a few years. Without Jake's help, she would have to fill that gap, but she was hoping she wouldn't have to. She found that she was excited at the prospect of seeing Jake in the next two or three weeks. She laid her head back against the tree, and the drowsiness began to take over...

A sound startled her into wakefulness, and she sat up suddenly against the tree trunk, straining to hear any further noises and searching her brain for what she had heard out there. It had been a snapping noise—someone stepping on a dry stick, maybe? She picked up the Winchester, eased to a standing position, and stared out toward the horses. It startled her to see that someone had untied her mare and mounted. He was weaving his way through the trees, away from their camp. She threw the Winchester up to her shoulder and snapped off a quick shot.

There was a loud shout, and the man tumbled off the horse, grabbing at his shoulder. Noise came from the undergrowth in front of her, maybe fifty yards away, and she levered the Winchester and fired another shot into the brush. She sheltered herself behind the pine tree and called to her horse, who was trotting away. The horse stopped and pawed the ground uncertainly. The noises she could hear now seemed to recede away from her, so she stayed behind the tree, not wanting to risk return fire.

Now she could hear someone, or maybe several people, running toward her from their campsite. Luke was the first to arrive. Julia waved to alert him to her position. He crouched and ran to her, motioning to Pete and Isaac behind him to stay where they were for the time being. All their horses were in view. Only her mare wasn't tethered, and she wasn't moving, so they waited for the sounds in front of them to fade away. After several minutes, they waved to Pete and Isaac to join them. Behind the boys, Ike was coming, holding a lantern in one hand.

They spread out and advanced toward the horses. Julia soothed the mare for a moment, then tethered her to the tree where she had been before. A quick examination showed that the other horses were unharmed. She pointed out to Ike where she had shot at the rider and seen him fall. Ike moved to the area and held up the lantern. There was blood on some leaves and underbrush around the spot where he had fallen. A clear trail of footprints and drops of blood led away from the horses. They found another set of footprints leading away in the underbrush where she had aimed the second shot. There was no blood there, so probably only one man had been wounded.

After several more minutes of searching the area and generally satisfying themselves that the horse thieves were gone, they brought the horses in closer to the camp and returned to join Jeanne, Irene, and the two little girls. Nobody seemed to be in the mood to sleep, so Julia made a pot of coffee, and they sat around the fire and talked until the sun rose. A quick breakfast followed. They agreed to double the guard on the horses until they had passed through the pine woods and reached more open ground.

———

Virgil Diehl leaned back in the cowhide-covered chair in his library and glared at the three men he was counting on to keep the use of the grazing land at the old Richardson place. He needed those 130 acres for grazing, sure, but there was more at stake than that. He owned more than a thousand acres, but he was grazing too many cows for his land, and he had done quite well by grazing several hundred acres on his neighbor's pastures, adjoining his land on three sides. He couldn't lose all of that grazing grass without selling off some of his herd, and that just wasn't in the plans. If this man McCabe stood up to him and wouldn't allow grazing, the other two ranchers might just do that as well. Then, there was the matter of the creek flowing across the old Richardson property and the pond. He needed that water.

Bull slumped in a chair in the corner, his nose covered in bandages. He was also sporting a black eye, and a whipped dog attitude. Diehl didn't intend to put up with that much longer. Bull was there to intimidate people. The fistfight had been shocking, Diehl had to admit. Bull had been thoroughly beaten and wasn't himself anymore. If Bull didn't snap out of it in the next few days, Diehl would send him packing. The man was no good to him like this.

His gaze swung over to Karras, the man he had hired for his skills with his gun, and Bates, the one he could generally count on to do whatever dirty work needed to be done. They had been the two that had been with the herd when McCabe chased them off. McCabe and somebody else in the woods, apparently. Diehl suspected it was the old codger who cleaned up in the saloon.

His glare settled on Karras. "I hired you for your six-shooters. You let him chase you off the land?"

A flush crept up Karras's neck and into his face. "He came out of the woods unexpected, I told you. Had his rifle on us already when we seen him. Had somebody else with a gun on us in the woods, too. Wasn't nothin' else we could do."

Diehl wasn't hearing anything he hadn't heard already, and he was completely out of patience. "Do something! Scare him off, but don't kill him unless it can look like an accident, or unless there is somebody we can blame it on." Daniels had an election coming, and he couldn't push the man too far right now. He needed the sheriff in his pocket. Karras stared at him blankly. Bull didn't even look up. Bates, he knew, had no good ideas.

Diehl, feeling exhausted, got up from his chair. "Get outta here," he scowled. "Come back in a couple days. I'll think of something." When they left, he dropped back into his chair. He had spent too much time building up this ranch to start selling and cutting down on his herd. He would think of a way to get rid of McCabe.

# CHAPTER 7

## OPENING SHOTS

The well-digging process had been a whole new experience for me. Boone put me on to a man from down the road in Kerrville who said he could tell if we had water down below. The foot of the bench on which they built the house seemed like the most promising spot. I knew we had water down at the creek, but a well near the house would make it a lot nicer. I had a feeling that the job of getting water would fall to Pete and Isaac, either way. When the well-man came, he walked around with a crooked stick, pointing it down at the ground. After he did that for a while, he told me he thought he could dig a well near the foot of the bench, as I'd hoped. He would give me two tries for twenty dollars.

I paid the man and stayed out of his way.

He brought out some kind of drill, which he stood upright and attached to a rig that was pulled by his horse. The horse walked around and around in circles. I watched for a while and got pretty bored, so pretty soon, I rode into town and looked up Boone in the saloon. He was always happy to take a break, especially since he knew I would buy. We swapped a few stories, and I bought the second round. Boone seemed to have something on his mind today, so I just waited for him to get around to it. Finally, he slammed down the second beer and leaned forward. "Jake," he said without further preamble, "folks like you around here."

"Okay," I said, after he lapsed back into silence. What he said didn't really surprise me, but I waited to see where he was going. He fidgeted around in his seat for a minute.

"You know," he said, "that Chase Daniels is up for re-election as sheriff." I nodded. "Folks don't like him," he said.

Now I saw where this was headed. "Nope." I shook my head emphatically. Boone slumped back in his chair. "There's nobody even gonna run against him. We need an honest sheriff, not somebody in Diehl's pocket." I eyed him for a minute, then waved for another round. "I've never been a sheriff. I have no idea how to be a sheriff. Why me?"

Boone took his time with that one. "I think it's 'cause they saw how you stood up to Diehl and Bull. An' it don't hurt none that you punched the stuffin's out of Bull." He chortled at that, clearly enjoying the memory. He waited while I thought that one over.

"I still know nothing about being a sheriff," I reminded him.

"You don't have to be no big-time gunfighter," he protested. "Just enforce the laws and treat people right. Everybody here will back you up." He stopped and watched my face. "Just tell me you'll think about it," he said finally. "It would mean a lot to the folks in the town." I agreed reluctantly to think about it, and finished my beer. After all, I didn't have a job and I was going to run out of money if I didn't get one soon. I mounted up and headed back to see what the well-digger was doing.

He was packing up and preparing to leave when I returned. He told me he had struck water at about fifty feet down. I didn't know if that was good or bad, but he seemed happy, so I took it as a good sign. He told me he would be back to widen out the hole in a few days and left. I walked over and peered down into the hole he had dug. I couldn't see anything, but I don't suppose you would, looking down fifty feet into the dark. I stood back and looked at the area around the hole. It would need a rock wall around it, and I could rig up a wooden structure above it with a rope on it. Then, I could tie a bucket on the end of the rope and crank it up and down for the water. I could do that after his work was done.

I walked back over to where I had tethered Sherman at the edge of the trees, untied him, gathered up the reins and was stepping up into the saddle when I heard a loud *crack* and felt a sharp sting across my right shoulder. I threw myself out of the saddle, keeping the horse between me and the direction of the shot. I yanked my Spencer from the scabbard, crouched, took my chances and sprinted, diving into the cover of the trees. A couple of shots followed, coming uncomfortably close.

I flattened myself in the underbrush, then slowly crawled to take shelter behind a large oak tree. I had plenty of experience at this sort of thing, unfortunately, both during the war and during my time at home in Kentucky. I knew that the biggest mistake I could make would be to move suddenly and expose my position. I lay completely still and searched the trees and brush in front of me and to both sides. Sherman was drifting toward me, then, to my relief, stopped and began cropping grass at the edge of the tree line. I didn't need him to give away my position. I looked longingly at the saddlebag, which I knew contained binoculars. I didn't dare go back for them.

Fifteen or twenty minutes went by without me so much as twitching a muscle. At the end of that time, I was pretty sure of two things: first, there were two of them out there—one across the pasture in the trees on my left, and the other on my side of the pasture. Second, they were both working to flank me and get closer to my position. I couldn't let them catch me in a crossfire, so I concentrated first on the one on my side of the pasture. Every few minutes, he worked his way closer in the underbrush, using trees for cover where they were available.

I watched his progress and concentrated on a thick clump of underbrush ahead and slightly to my right. The trees thinned out a bit at that spot, and I was pretty sure he was going to have to use that underbrush as cover if he was foolish enough to keep coming closer. I could mark his progress by the occasional quiver of twigs and leaves. When his trail of progress reached that clump I was looking at, I moved a bit to my right, using the oak tree as shelter from the man on my left. I rose quickly and fired three quick shots in the underbrush, first left, then center, then right. After the third shot I heard a sharp cry, then a muffled oath. A few shots thudded into the oak tree from across the pasture, but I paid that no mind.

I kneeled down to protect myself against return fire from in front and watched the underbrush sharply. After a minute or two of silence, the branches shook, and I could clearly hear someone dragging himself away in the other direction. Now and then, he came clearly into view, and I had a shot, but didn't take it. They may have been out only to scare me—they had me dead to rights swinging into the saddle. That may have been a bad shot, or it may have been on purpose. I chose to believe the latter.

My remaining problem was the guy on my left across the pasture, which narrowed considerably before it reached the well and the cabin behind me. If he were a good shot and well hidden over there, I might still have a problem. I searched the woods for any sign of him, but came up empty. I reached down and picked up a rock, tossing it into the brush off to my right. He went for the bait and rose slightly, firing two shots into the brush. I used the moment to dart into a spot behind two trees in front of me, trunks growing closely together. I reached them before he stopped firing at the brush to my right.

I could see him pretty clearly now. His clothing was dark, but he had given himself away with movement. It exposed his whole left side from the waist up. Bracing the Spencer against the trunk of one tree, I aimed for the outer half of his left shoulder and slowly squeezed off the shot. He staggered backward, clutching at his left shoulder and dropping his rifle. He bent to pick it up, then ran away from me, zig-zagging through the trees. I let him go. As woodsmen, I thought, I was going to have to give both of them failing grades.

The one I had just winged reached his horse, jumped aboard, and took off to the north, toward the Diehl ranch. I had a pretty good idea that was who had put these two up to this clumsy attempt to drive me off. I waited another ten minutes in case there was someone else, but nothing stirred out there. I walked forward to the underbrush where I had shot the first man. There was an obvious trail of blood—clear, but not a really heavy trail. I was guessing it was more than a scratch, but not fatal. The blood trail also led off toward the Diehl ranch.

I retraced my steps, remembering then the sting across my shoulder. I took off my shirt and looked at it. This one was just a scratch. I pulled a clean rag from my saddlebag and held it against the wound for a few minutes until the bleeding stopped. Then I walked Sherman up the trail and over to the cabin. I reassured myself that nothing had been disturbed at the cabin, then mounted up and rode toward Fredericksburg.

———

Julia rode alongside the wagon and looked in at her mother, now riding in the back of the wagon. Isaac held an umbrella over her for shade, but Jeanne was tossing back and forth, sweating and wincing as the wagon hit bumps in the road. Things had finally reached the point where Jeanne could no longer refuse to ride in the back. She didn't have the strength to ride up front anymore, and her fever was getting worse.

Ike glanced in the back and pulled the wagon over to the side. Julia rode up to him. Luke, behind them, pulled their wagon over and walked up to join the conversation. Ike tied off the reins and leaned forward, elbows on his knees, shaking his head. He looked up at Julia. "We have to find a doctor for her and stop," he said. "I know she doesn't want us to stop, but we have to." Julia nodded vigorously, tears forming in her eyes. Ike looked over at

Luke. "We don't expect you and your family to wait with us, if you need to go on."

Luke hesitated only a moment. "Irene and I talked it over this morning," he said. "We'll stay with you. Please find her a doctor and don't fret about us."

Ike pulled out a hand-drawn map the ferry owner had given him and studied it. "I think the next town we're coming to is named Tyler. We'll look for a doctor in Tyler." He looked over his shoulder at his wife in the back of the wagon. Sweat was trickling down her face, and she stared up at him blankly. Ike picked up the reins and clucked at the horses to get going. "The sooner, the better," he mumbled to himself.

———

Two days later, Julia left the doctor's office in Tyler and wandered across the road to a peach orchard. Marveling at the number of peaches, she saw that most weren't yet ripe, and contented herself with wandering through the rows of trees. A feeling of helplessness almost over-whelmed her. She had no idea how to help. It just seemed important to be near her mother. "Have one." Julia jumped in surprise. She wheeled to see a man offering a ripe peach. She thanked him and retreated from the orchard.

Re-entering the doctor's office, she saw Ike talking to the doctor, a white-haired man, probably in his sixties. She joined the conversation.

"I dealt with a lot of fevers during the war," he was telling Ike. "I don't think any of the treatments we tried back then really worked. We still don't have a real good way to deal with it. Best thing I know is to keep her quiet and wrapped up in some cold towels. We'll know more in a day or two." He turned and went back into his office.

Ike started back toward Jeanne's bedside when Julia stopped him with a hand on his arm. "You were up with her all night, Dad. Let me take a turn and you get some sleep."

Ike nodded and hobbled out of the office without a word.

Late that night, dozing in a chair at her mother's bedside, Julia was awakened when Jeanne tossed in the bed, muttering to herself and throwing off the towels wrapped around her. Julia jumped up and was alarmed to see sweat pouring down her mother's face. She ran to the door and shouted for the doctor. He emerged from an upstairs room a couple minutes later, pulling on a robe and donning his spectacles. He hurried down the stairs and over to Jeanne's bedside.

"Best thing that could have happened," she heard him mumble. He pulled dry towels from a cupboard in the corner and used them to wipe Jeanne's face. After another ten minutes of tossing and mumbling, she seemed to settle down, then drifted back off to sleep.

Julia had remained silent the entire time, letting the doctor work. Finally, she had to ask: "What's happening?"

The doctor shrugged, then took another look at Jeanne. "I think she'll be fine now," he said. "The fever is likely to be gone when she wakes up."

———

After staying in Tyler for two more days to allow Jeanne to regain some strength, the two families started off again. Jeanne rode in the wagon's front again, and Julia noticed she had regained some color and strength. She joined in conversations and seemed to look forward to reaching their destination. As her mother regained strength, Ike regained his indomitable outlook and cheerfulness. It was the first time Julia had felt good about the move since the day the ferry had exploded at the Mississippi River.

Several days later, they reached the town of Waco and the biggest bridge Julia had ever seen. A suspension bridge hung over a broad river flowing past them. In answer to her question to a passerby, she was told it was the Brazos River. She stared at the large brick structures on either side of the river, with a suspension bridge hanging in between. Julia had her doubts about crossing the bridge with the wagon and horses, but while they waited, a herd of cattle crossed over. If a herd of cattle can cross, she thought, so can we. As they lined up at the foot of the bridge, she decided to ignore all the swinging and swaying the bridge was doing as people and animals crossed.

After about the longest fifteen minutes Julia could ever remember, they all stood on the other side of the bridge. The bridge had swayed unbelievably, but somehow, nobody had fallen off, including herself. She heaved a sigh of relief. In another fifteen minutes, it was time to say goodbye to the Jackson family. They had only a brief journey south from this point to reach Luke's brother's farm. The two families milled about for a few minutes, giving hugs and saying goodbye. Julia was sad to see them go, but reminded herself they were very close to reaching their own destination.

They pushed on for a few more hours after leaving

the Jacksons and finally made camp in a meadow just a few hundred yards away from the trail. After a quick dinner, Julia pulled out a map Jake had sent her, and they all looked to familiarize themselves with this last leg of the trip. It occurred to Julia that she didn't know how to find Jake or their land after reaching Fredericksburg. She mentioned that to the family.

"I suppose," she said, "that we could just ask at the post office or general store and see if anybody knows the best way to find him. He said the land is a little north of the town, but I think it would be better to find Jake first. Maybe there is a café where we could ask."

Her father chuckled loudly. "First place I'm going to stop is the saloon. I'll bet they know Jake there. I'll bet that's the first place he stopped." Jeanne rolled her eyes, but Julia couldn't suppress a chuckle. Ike was probably right about that.

# CHAPTER 8

## RUNNING FOR OFFICE

Diehl leaned against the rail of his back porch and stared at his henchmen in disgust. Karras had his shoulder heavily bandaged, and along with Bates, had just been attended to by the town doctor. Bates had his leg wrapped up and walked with a cane. Hobbled with a cane, more like it. Karras still had his gun hand available, but Bates wouldn't be any good for weeks. Not that they'd been much use to him lately.

Diehl fixed his glare on both of them as they stood in the yard below the porch. "This was worse than last time. He put a bullet in both of you, and you got nothin' to show for it?"

Karras shifted on his feet and looked over at Bates. "You said just to scare him off," he reminded Diehl. "We weren't tryin' to hit him."

Diehl's face turned an even deeper color of red. "And after he shot you, were you trying then?" Karras stared at his feet and said nothing.

"There's another family, going to move onto that

land," Diehl said, his voice rising a couple octaves higher. "More people to run off."

Karras stirred himself and tried again. "They're just farmers, I think," he offered. "Shouldn't be no trouble."

"No trouble?" Diehl shouted. "You can't handle even one man by himself!" Karras went back to saying nothing. Bates had wisely remained silent the entire time. "Get out!" Diehl waved them off and went back in the ranch house, the door slamming emphatically behind him.

Several cabinets were opened and slammed shut in the dining room. A maid stuck her head around the corner and quickly retreated. Diehl finally found what he was looking for—a large bottle of whiskey. He poured a generous amount for himself and collapsed into a large side chair. He took a few minutes to numb himself and cool off, then considered his situation. Bull was gone—he had just pulled his freight and left about a week ago. He wasn't of much use the way he'd been acting lately, but Diehl could have still thrown the name around to scare people. Well, if word hadn't gotten around yet, maybe he could still threaten somebody here or there by threatening to send Bull around for a visit.

The water on the old Richardson property was a must. He didn't have enough water to sustain his herd. This guy McCabe, he had to admit, grudgingly, was a fighter. He was apparently a crack shot with the rifle, and he had completely out-maneuvered Karras and Bates in the woods out there. With a new family coming in to claim the land, he was running out of time. Diehl sighed and went to top off his glass.

Collapsing into his favorite cowhide-covered chair, he thought about what he needed to do. To make things worse, Daniels, the sheriff, had told him that McCabe was running for sheriff in the election, coming up in just a few weeks. If he had Karras or somebody kill McCabe in a dry-gulch shooting, or with a shot in the back, Daniels probably couldn't cover that one up. Diehl didn't need the Texas Rangers sticking their noses into the middle of this. A range war, or maybe a straight-up gunfight with witnesses, one of those might work. Maybe, he thought, he would need both.

The thing is, he reminded himself, he knew a gunfighter. A good one. Maybe the man used some dirty tricks, but what did Diehl care about that? He'd used the man's services a time or two in the past. He got up and crossed the room to pull out a desk drawer. He began rummaging around through the papers and various items of clutter in the drawer. After about thirty seconds, he emerged from his search and scanned the piece of paper he was holding. Vincent, that was the name. Al Vincent. Maybe Vincent would know of three or four others that might be useful in a range war with this new family moving in. Vincent was located in Paris, Texas. He could be here in a few days.

Diehl mounted up and rode into town, ignoring the greeting or two that came his way. He pulled up in front of the telegraph office. A small, nervous clerk named Adams stood behind the desk and waited while Diehl scratched out his message, then surveyed what he had written:

*Vincent:*

*Need your services. Same kind of job as before. Stop.*

> *Need maybe four others to persuade squatters to get off my land. You know the kind of people I'll need.*
> *Stop.*
>
> *Same pay as last time. Bonus for quick results.*
> *Stop.*
>
> *Diehl.*

He handed the note to the clerk who read it, swallowed a couple times and sent the message. Diehl fixed him with a stare when he had finished. "I need you to have a short memory about this."

Adams nodded.

"A very short memory," he emphasized.

Adams nodded again. "Yes, sir."

Diehl stared at him for another ten or fifteen seconds. Finally, satisfied, he turned to leave. "I think we understand each other," he said. "I'd hate for Bull to pay you a visit."

The door slammed behind him.

———

I stood back and surveyed my work on the well. I had built a waist-high rock wall around it. The bucket and rope were in place. I had used them to pull several buckets of water up from the new well, twisting the crank to lift the bucket. I had brought a barrel and put it behind the cabin. I planned to fill up the barrel so there would be water on hand when Julia and the family arrived. I had kept a wary eye on the pasture out there behind me as I worked on the well. The wall around the well would serve as protection against another attack, but

I didn't plan to stop there. Some defensive positions needed to be built around this place.

I was having some second thoughts now about placing Julia and her family in this situation. We could, I thought, wind up with a range war in progress when they got into town. I decided I would tell them first thing when they arrived about everything that had happened. If they didn't want the property, I could buy it from them and help them find another place. I was a bit lost in these thoughts when I heard a rustle in the underbrush off to my right. I took a couple of casual steps away from the noise, then grabbed my Spencer and dropped behind the wall as I threw down with the rifle.

Boone lifted his hands in the air. "Easy, Pilgrim. I ain't seen you in town for a couple days, so I came out to see what you've been doin'." He surveyed my work on the well with an approving eye. "Nice well. Assumin' it has water in it."

I shook my head and chuckled. "It has water. You plan to make yourself useful out here, or just annoy me?"

He shrugged. "Both, I guess." His eyes dropped to my waist. "You went for the Spencer instead of the pistol," he observed. "You been practicing with the Colt? You might not have time to get to that rifle sometimes." Well, now he had succeeded in annoying me, but I knew he was right.

"I've practiced," I said defensively.

He set down a burlap bag he had been carrying over his shoulder, then began taking out some beer bottles. He set up the bottles along a fallen tree limb. "Let's see you hit these," he said.

I walked over and stood about twenty-five yards away from the bottles, then pulled the Colt and fired at them.

Three of the six bottles shattered, but the other three were still standing. Boone clucked at me reprovingly.

"Gonna take some more practice, pilgrim." He replaced the three broken bottles, then backed away from them. "Square up to your target a little better. Make the draw a little smoother. Slow down if you have to, but hit what you're aimin' at."

I took his advice and tried again. This time, I hit five of the six bottles. He nodded approvingly, then pointed at the bag with more bottles in it. "Make good use of those," he told me. He looked around him. "What d'ya want me to make myself useful at?"

I walked over to the place where I had taken cover the other day, pointing out to him where my attackers had come from. "I want to build a defensive position here," I told him. "Help me drag a couple big logs in here so I can take cover if I need to."

Boone followed me over, and we dragged three logs and positioned them. We dragged two more over and laid them at a ninety-degree angle to the first two in order to give protection from the left for any shots coming from across the pasture. I pulled a few branches in front of the logs to make the barrier harder to see from a distance. I stood back and surveyed the defensive position we had created. I was satisfied with it. I would have been pretty happy for it when Diehl's men had attacked me a couple days ago.

Boone watched me silently. "I just done you a favor," he said. "Several favors, actually."

I had to agree with that statement. I knew he would get around to his point, so I just waited.

"Today's the last day you can register for the sheriff's election in a few weeks," he said.

I waved my arm in frustration. "I told you I know nothing about being a sheriff." Boone shrugged. "So, you can learn." I shook my head back and forth emphatically. "Why should I?"

Boone watched me for a minute, then leaned over and spit into the underbrush. "Lemme ask you a question. Do you think Diehl will get one of his goons to attack you in town again?"

I thought it likely and told him so.

Boone nodded. "So, here's one more question for you. When that happens, do you want Daniels to come after you and try to arrest you again, or would you rather be the sheriff when it happens? You can't expect there'll be folks around to back Diehl and Daniels off ever' time. Besides, as far as I can tell, you need a job."

I thought that one over, and though I didn't want to admit it, Boone made a lot of sense. I put up one last excuse: "I have no idea how to register."

Boone's face split into a grin. He had me, and he knew it. "Well," he drawled, "ain't you the lucky one. I asked around this mornin' and I know just what you need to do."

I threw my hands up in resignation and followed him over to the horses.

When we reached the road to Fredericksburg, I moved Sherman up to trot alongside Boone. "Where are we going?" I asked.

Boone pointed ahead to the cluster of buildings that was Fredericksburg. "Right there," he said. "Fredericksburg is the county seat for Gillespie County."

I stared at him in amazement.

"Okay," he admitted. "I just found that out this mornin'. Anyway, you can register at the courthouse."

We tied up the horses outside the two-story court-house and walked in. Boone steered me toward a clerk behind a desk in a corner of the first floor. The clerk looked at me as I walked up, then glanced at Boone, who gave me a little nudge forward.

"This here is Jake McCabe," he said.

The clerk brightened up visibly. He pulled out a sheet of paper and smoothed it on the table in front of him. "McCabe for sheriff," he mumbled to himself. He pulled out a pen and a pot of ink. "Mr. McCabe," he said, "let me fill this out for you."

I nodded, and he asked a few questions. "Full name?"

"Jacob Matthew McCabe."

"Age?"

"Thirty," I told him.

We continued on for a few more questions. Reading the sheet upside-down, I could see him pause at the question, *Resident?*

I had been wondering if I qualified on that count. I had been here only a few weeks and owned no property. He glanced up at me. "Do you live here?"

I said, "Yes."

He checked the box. I glanced over at Boone. "We need us a new sheriff," he explained. The clerk checked off a few more boxes, listed my address as the post office, and stamped the sheet when he was done.

"Congratulations, Mr. McCabe," he said, extending his hand. "You are a candidate for Sheriff of Gillespie County."

We walked out and stood on the steps of the court-house. I looked over at Boone. "Was that legal?" I asked. Boone looked hurt. "Of course, it was legal. We just didn't want to get hung up on no details, that's all."

It saved me from thinking about that one very much when I saw Diehl's gunman, Karras, coming toward me. He stopped in front of me, glancing over at Boone, then at the courthouse behind us.

"You don't want to run against Daniels for sheriff," he said. I took a step closer. "Just did it," I told him. "Just got done registering."

He backed up a step. "That was a mistake," he said. He was trying to look threatening, but I could see a bit of fear in his eyes. I walked in on him, and he kept backing up until he came up against one of the courthouse pillars. I glanced down at his left shoulder. His sleeve covered it, but it appeared to be thick with bandages underneath. I reached out and gave it a hard squeeze. Karras blanched.

"Don't threaten me," I told him. I took a step back. His hand hovered over his gun, but I was too close. His look at me was filled with venom. I doubled up my right fist and waited. He brushed past me, trotted over to his horse and rode away.

I rejoined Boone and watched Karras ride out of town. "What happens now?" I asked.

"I start talkin' to everybody that comes in the saloon and all the store owners," he said. "Bull left town, by the way. This is gonna work." I walked over to Sherman and mounted up. "Jake," he called. I swung my horse around and waited. "Keep practicing with that six-shooter," he advised.

———

It was the second day since they had parted ways with the Jackson family. Julia rode alongside the family, weary of the journey and scanning the horizon constantly for any sign of Fredericksburg. She saw a river winding in front of them, and her hopes rose. If this was the Guadalupe River, they were very close. They reached the water, and Pete began scouting downriver, looking for a narrow, shallow area where they could make a crossing with the wagon. She waited impatiently.

In about twenty minutes, Pete returned, saying he had found a place to cross. More importantly, he had seen wagon wheel tracks, giving them all comfort that the wagon could ford successfully. When they reached the crossing, Julia secured a rope from her saddle horn to the wagon tongue, then led off across the river. They waded in, finding the water surprisingly deep but calm. Julia's feet in the stirrups just touched the water before they climbed. Pete and Isaac brought up the rear, prepared to jump in and push if need be, but the wagon climbed up steadily and rolled up on the opposite bank.

The rest was short—they were all eager to reach town. Julia led off again, taking in rolling, verdant hills. No wonder Jake had said it would remind her a little of home. As the sun sank lower in the west, she spotted a few deer feeding in the valleys. Finally, cresting a rise and shielding her eyes against the sun, she saw a small cluster of buildings in the distance. She consulted the map Jake had sent while the wagon pulled up alongside. She pointed excitedly at the town while Ike supplied the words she was thinking in his booming voice, "We're home!"

Forty-five minutes later, she reined in her horse next to a wooden sign with the single word she had been looking for *Fredericksburg*. She couldn't believe they had finally arrived. She looked back in the wagon where Ike was laughing excitedly. There was a sparkle in her mother's eyes Julia hadn't seen in a long time. This could be, she thought, just the thing her mother had needed. There was hope for the future here. Behind the wagon, Pete and Isaac were waving their hats in the air and whooping.

As they moved along Main Street, they could hear Ike loud and clear, announcing that the saloon was the first stop for him. It didn't take long to spot a saloon sign, and Ike pulled the wagon to the side. Julia dismounted and tethered her horse. She didn't plan to go into the saloon, but she couldn't imagine denying Ike what he'd been looking forward to for weeks. She always wanted to give him a hand when he climbed down from the wagon, but she knew he wouldn't hear of it. She stood to the side while he worked his way down and grabbed his crutch.

As Ike walked toward the saloon, a homespun-looking man in perhaps his early sixties came to the batwing doors and shaded his eyes against the sun while he surveyed the newcomers to town. He chuckled as he pushed through the doors and approached the wagon.

"You'd be the Hawkins family," he announced to no one in particular. He walked over to her father. "Ike," the man said. "Welcome." He swept off his raggedy hat and semi-bowed to Jeanne. "Ma'am," he intoned solemnly, "I'm Boone. I'm from the same neck of the woods you folks are from. Hat still in hand, he walked over and semi-bowed again. "Julia," he said, "you're even prettier than Jake said you was."

Julia's face broke into an ear-to-ear smile. "You know Jake?"

Boone straightened up and jammed the hat back on his head.

"Know him?" he crowed. "I taught that pilgrim

what's what around here. Hep'd him build that cabin of your'n. Watched his back in a couple scrapes, I did."

Julia's smile faded. "Scrapes?" Boone waved his hand dismissively.

"Nothing Jake couldn't handle. We love him around here. He's gonna be our new sheriff, I'm telling ye." He turned toward the saloon. "Y'all come in and set," he said.

"Right behind you!" Ike announced and followed Boone up the steps. Jeanne quickly declined, then stopped Pete and Isaac as they were eagerly following their father.

"You boys stay here," she blurted. "You're too young." Boone paused on the boardwalk and looked back at Julia.

"You come too," he said. "Won't nobody bother you. We know how to treat ladies in Texas."

Julia hesitated only a moment, then the smile returned to her face. "I don't mind if I do," she said, then followed them inside.

# CHAPTER 9

## REUNITED

Diehl sat in his study, leaning back in his cowhide-covered chair, trying to figure out just how serious Karras was about his offer to kill McCabe. Karras stood awkwardly in front of the enormous stone fireplace, a trifle pale, occasionally grabbing his injured left shoulder, his dark eyes boring into Diehl. "You want him dead, right? I'll take care of it."

Diehl studied his face. The man seemed serious about this. "Why the change, Karras? You sounded like you were just toying with him in the woods the other day. Did he do something else to you?"

Karras's face flushed, and his eyes flashed with anger. "Let's just say I don't like him, and maybe I want him gone as much as you do." He bit the words off slowly and evenly, his eyes locked in on Diehl.

Diehl remained silent for a moment, toying absently with a pocketknife he kept on the desk to open letters. Clearly, McCabe had angered Karras personally. He would find out what that was after Karras left. Meanwhile, this anger could be a useful thing to him. It just needed to be directed in a way that didn't point back to Diehl personally.

"Just what is it you plan to do, Karras? This can't be tied in with me or the water on that pasture over there. It's a troublesome time right now, what with the election for sheriff and all." He watched while Karras debated his answer.

Karras shifted uncomfortably on his feet, staring past Diehl, out the window. Finally, he shifted his focus back to Diehl. "It won't be around here," he said finally.

"Not good enough, Karras." Diehl leaned forward. "I need to know more. How do you plan to get him away from here? How would you do it?"

Karras mumbled something under his breath.

"Can't hear you!" Diehl was growing angry now. "I want to know your plan, and I want it now."

Karras seemed to come to his decision. "That horse of his. He's pretty attached to it. I, uh, borrow his horse and lead him on a chase. Then I take him down."

Diehl leaned back and thought about that for a minute. "Then you take him down? You going to shoot him from ambush? Dry-gulch him?"

Karras's eyes were on the floor. Slowly, he raised them to look at Diehl. "No way, boss. Fair fight. I'll take him, no problem."

Diehl's gut told him that was a lie, as Karras was a weasel at heart. Diehl didn't particularly care, though. "Not within fifty miles of here, do you hear me? Better yet, make sure you're out of this county."

Karras nodded, jammed his hat on his head and turned for the door. "You got it. Out of this county."

Diehl watched him go, deciding whether this changed anything he'd planned for Al Vincent and his men when they arrived. Maybe Karras could handle McCabe and maybe he couldn't. McCabe was a pretty salty customer. Besides, somebody still needed to drive the new family off the property, and Diehl didn't really have anybody left to get the job done. Having McCabe out of town would come in handy. If Karras couldn't handle him, he would have Vincent get the job done later. Satisfied, he went looking for that bottle of whiskey he kept handy.

———

I rode into Fredericksburg, thinking that a meal at the café sounded good. I had spent the afternoon hauling fallen trees up to the plateau, then used the axe to split firewood. I had read that Abraham Lincoln had been a log splitter. I didn't envy him the job. I rode up to the café, lost in my thoughts, and dismounted. Just as I tied Sherman to the rail, I heard somebody yelling, "Mr. McCabe!". I spun around and saw Pete and Isaac sprinting toward me. They hit me with a bearhug and knocked me back into the hitching rail. "Easy!" I said, laughing. "And just call me Jake. When did you guys get here?" They told me they had ridden in just about a half hour ago. I looked around, seeing the wagon with Jeanne, who waved at me. I waved back but kept looking, searching for Julia.

"She's in the saloon," said Pete, grinning at me. I chuckled. That boy was getting too wise for his own good.

I crossed the street to give Jeanne a hug and a kiss on the cheek. We exchanged a few words, and I heard foot-steps behind me. I turned around just in time to get knocked backward a second time. Julia had launched herself from the saloon porch. I staggered back and luckily managed to get my balance. We hugged for a long time, and she gave me a quick kiss. This was an even better reception than I'd imagined. I didn't seem to want to put her down, so I searched my brain for something to say. "Welcome to Fredericksburg," I offered lamely.

She laughed and gave me another kiss. "You can put me down now," she told me. Then she took my hand. "Let's go see Dad."

I followed her back into the saloon.

Ike let out a shout when he saw me and waved us over to the table. He and Boone seemed to have hit it off, judging by the number of empty beer glasses I could see. And to think they had only been here for a half hour. We sat at the table with them. Boone seemed to be in the middle of a very tall tale, which Ike was clearly enjoying. Julia sat next to me and filled me in on their trip. My trip had been pretty uneventful compared to theirs. I told her there had been a little trouble with one of their new neighbors, and I needed to talk to them about it. She touched my eye and cheek, where the bruises from the fight with Bull had finally faded to a mottled yellow color.

"I was wondering about this," she said. I promised to explain what was going on to all of them when we had a chance.

Eventually, either Boone ran out of stories, or Ike had heard enough of them for the time being. I couldn't really tell which, but I'd never heard Boone run out of stories, so I had a pretty good idea which it was. The family had been eating campfire food for a couple months, so I offered to buy dinner at the café, and they all seemed pretty happy with that idea. Over dinner, I described the land, and they were eager to see it. I went ahead and told them about the neighbor, Diehl, my fight with Bull, and the ambush I had run into. I was reading their expressions as I talked. The boys didn't seem to know what to think. Julia was watching my face without expression, and Jeanne looked troubled by it. Ike was an old campaigner, and he looked ready to fight. I finished what I had to say and suggested they talk about it. They went to stay at the hotel in town for the night, and they agreed that I would take them out to see the land and cabin first thing in the morning.

Julia stayed outside with me for a while longer after the others had gone in.

"What would you do, Jake?" she asked me. "Would you keep the land or sell and find a place more peaceful? And do you really want the property if we decide not to keep it?"

I didn't need long to think that one over. "I'm a fighter in a situation like this," I said. "That land is worth keeping, and I'd fight for it. Already have fought for it. That's just me. You'll need to decide what you want to do." I thought for a moment. "There's one other thing I forgot to mention. The sheriff sides with Diehl. He's probably getting paid by Diehl. Don't let me forget to tell Ike."

She nodded, studying my face. "And if you're the sheriff?" she asked. "Boone said he thinks you're going to be the sheriff soon."

It surprised me she'd heard that already. I shrugged, then shook my head. "It's true, I'm running for sheriff," I agreed. "But I expect little to come of it. Boone talked me into it, and I did it because the sheriff we have here is crooked—just does what Diehl wants. Probably gets paid by Diehl."

She smiled. "Don't count yourself out, Jake. You're a good man. People like you. I like you." She raised up on her tiptoes and gave me a kiss and a pat on the cheek. Then she went inside.

———

I could see immediately that the Hawkins family was very impressed with the property I had bought for them. We toured the cabin—it didn't have any furniture in it, but it was a bit bigger than what they'd had back in Kentucky, and as a temporary home, they professed themselves delighted with it. We rode down to the pasture and discussed how many head of cattle this grass would support. I was guessing with the rich grass and good water, it might support fifty to sixty cows. Of course, they had come to file for the 1,280-acre grant, which would support ten times that number. That led to questions about how close to this land they could obtain a grant. Ike lifted his eyes up to the north and pointed. "Is that Diehl's land?" I nodded.

Ike reined his horse around. "Let's go back to the cabin and talk," he suggested.

We rode single-file back up to the plateau. Jeanne took a blanket and spread it on the ground outside the cabin. Ike chuckled and jerked a thumb in the direction of the cabin door.

"Got to get some furniture. We can sleep on the floor with blankets until we get that going. He looked back out over the pasture, then pointed down to the well. Can't thank you enough for the cabin and the well. I want to see if we can get a grant close to here. We want you to join us, Jake."

Julia slid her arm through mine, and there were murmurs of agreement from the rest of the family. I mumbled my appreciation, and I seemed to be getting a little misty-eyed. It saved me from having to elaborate on my answer when Boone rode up.

A grin slowly spread across Ike's face. "A useful man, that," he said. "Where does he live, Jake?"

I explained that he slept in the back room of the saloon in exchange for some light duties. "Hmmm..." Ike stroked his chin thoughtfully.

"He says he doesn't like punching cows," I warned Ike.

He chuckled again. "Maybe he just needs a little something to work for," he said. "Maybe a little land to call his own would change his mind."

We all sat down on the blanket. Ike glanced around at his family, then announced abruptly: "We want to keep this place. Jake, Boone, tell us what we need to do to defend it. I got a couple ideas myself, but I want to hear from you. Boone and I exchanged glances, then I explained about the defensive position I had built down below. I also told them I thought we should stack logs and branches behind the cabin, near the edge of the plateau. We could shelter behind it and use the higher ground to defend both the cabin behind it, and the pastureland below it."

A moment of silence followed, then Boone spoke up: "If'n I was you, I'd have one lookout posted ever' night up here at one of those piles of logs. I'll take a turn myself."

Ike nodded, then looked over his shoulder at the

entrance to the property from the road. "What about somebody comin' from the road?" he asked.

It was decided to cut a hole or two in the cabin wall on that side to use for a gun port. Ike pronounced himself satisfied on that score.

"Now," he said finally, "do either of you know anything about filing for one of those grants?"

I shook my head no, but Boone surprised me, not for the first time. "I done some askin' at the courthouse," he informed us. "You got to go to Austin and apply at the Texas General Land Office. Don't know exackly where that is in Austin," he added as an afterthought. He leaned back on his elbows, clearly pleased with himself.

Ike slapped his hands together with delight. "Boone," he thundered, "after we get us some more land, you got to come out here and stake yourself a spot out here. We'll have a few acres to spare," he finished.

Boone surprised me once again by not turning down the offer. "You'll never get rid of him at your dinner table," I mumbled. Boone turned injured eyes in my direction, but everybody else ignored me. I decided to contribute something useful.

"You must at least explain that you're a Confederate veteran," I reminded him. "I don't know how you can prove that. Bring the papers I gave you from the bank to prove you own some land here. Your war wounds..." I gestured at his leg.

"I've still got a paper they gave me when I signed up for the army," he said. "I'll bring that too. Jake," Ike continued, "would you come to Austin with Julia and me to look into this grant? Tomorrow, I'm thinking."

I agreed.

"Boone," he asked, "would you help the boys and Jeanne keep an eye on this place while we're gone?"

Boone nodded. He pointed at some tools the boys had unloaded from their wagon. "I'll start knockin' together some bed frames," he promised.

"Dinner table first," Jeanne said.

Jeanne disappeared into the cabin while Ike, Boone, and the two boys began to work at building a dining table for the cabin. I stood to join them, but Julia took me by the hand and led me down to the water well, then over to look at the fortification Boone and I had built there. After a moment, she turned to put her arms around my waist, then leaned back to look me in the eye.

"This is wonderful," she said. "It is everything any of us had hoped for."

I looked at her doubtfully. "Even Jeanne?" I asked.

She nodded her head emphatically. "Maybe Mom most of all," she said. "She's showing more energy and excitement than I've ever seen from her. I think it's because she can see a wonderful future for her kids here."

I nodded slowly. That started to make a lot of sense to me. Maybe my mother would have felt the same way if we could have escaped that senseless feud a few years ago and come out here.

"Sure," I said after a moment. "I get it. Maybe my folks and Russell..." my voice trailed off.

Julie raised one hand to the back of my head and pulled me down for a kiss. After a moment, I could hear snickering. We turned to see Pete and Isaac at the well, drawing up some water. Julia scolded them, but she was laughing at the same time. We walked back up the hill and pitched in to help with that table.

---

Karras stood in the bunkhouse and tossed a few things into his bag. Diehl would never follow up on exactly how he would take care of McCabe, he was sure, so that left him free to do what he wanted. He felt sure he could take McCabe in a straight-up gunfight, but why bother when he could just take the sure thing? Nobody would miss McCabe, anyway. He had scouted the road leading north and east to Waco, and there were several places where he could shoot the man while he was on the trail. All he needed was for McCabe to follow him north on that road. Stealing the horse should do the trick. He would have to let the horse go free after the shooting, though. That way, nobody could prove that he did the killing. If he got caught with the horse, they would hang him. Too bad. It looked like a good horse.

Karras left the bunkhouse, looking around to see if anybody was watching. Everybody was working the cattle, except for Bates, who was still gimping around on a cane. With Bates laid up and Bull gone, Diehl didn't have anybody left to do his dirty work. Karras had heard that Diehl had sent for a few gunfighters from Paris, Texas, and a frown crossed his face as he saddled up his horse. Diehl was a jerk, but he paid well and the work had been pretty easy. He didn't really want to lose his job. He swung up on his horse and rode out of the corral. After he had taken care of McCabe, maybe Diehl would still have a place for him.

He was pretty leery of coming up on the McCabe land through the woods these days. He had to admit, grudgingly, that the man was pretty good with the rifle, and he was pretty good at sneaking up on people out there among the trees. Karras took the road toward the Hawkins property, planning to get off the road when he was close to the cabin. He would try working his way up to that makeshift corral on foot. Rounding a bend, he saw dust being raised on the road in front of him. He immediately pulled off into the trees and dismounted, waiting to see who was coming.

As the object in front of him drew closer, he could see that it was a wagon, being pulled by two horses. He muzzled his horse with a bandanna and waited. When the wagon was maybe fifty yards off, he could see three people riding on the bench seat. He squinted through the dust as the wagon pulled even with him. McCabe was driving, the girl was next to him, and the old man with only one good leg rode on the other side. They pulled on past and disappeared down the road. A big smile crossed Karras's face. This would be easier than he had thought.

# CHAPTER 10

# BAITING THE TRAP

We topped a rise, and the buildings of Austin came into view. It was a little smaller than I had expected, and I had to confess I knew little about the town. Julia had been reading local newspapers and filled us in on what she knew. I was aware it was the capital of Texas, but Julia said that had only been decided for good in a state-wide vote just a couple months before. Because of that vote and the coming of the Houston and Texas Central railway, also just a few months ago, they expected Austin to grow a lot during the coming years. As we rolled into town, I could see a lot of old wooden buildings being replaced by stone and brick structures. Seeing all those buildings going up so close to each other made me think I had done the right thing in riding on past Austin before picking a place to live. I didn't like big towns.

We asked a couple folks for directions and found our way to the Texas General Land Office building. It wasn't much to look at from the outside, but according to Boone, that's where we had to go to apply for the land grant. We decided to get a bite to eat at the café across the street before going inside. Seated at the table, Ike spread out the papers he had brought with him. The paper showing his enlistment in the CSA army seemed like all he would need to prove he was a veteran. We weren't really sure how much proof they would ask for in terms of residency and disabled status, but there was only one way to find out. We finished eating, crossed the street and pushed open the doors at the Land Office.

We were greeted and shown to a desk where a man in some sort of rolling chair told us to take a seat. I could see with a quick glance that he didn't have his legs. He glanced with sympathy as Ike worked his way across the room with his one-arm crutch and took a seat.

"We're here about the land grant for veterans," Ike informed him. He glanced down at Ike's leg, then back up.

"I assume the grant is for you, sir?" he asked Ike.

"It is," Ike agreed. The man reached for a pen and some paper.

"Can I ask where you sustained your wound, sir?"

"Shiloh, second day, Hood's corps," Ike said simply.

The clerk dipped his pen in some ink and began writing. He asked Ike's full name and made a note that he had lost a leg in Hood's corps at the Battle of Shiloh.

He referenced a document he had pulled from a drawer as he asked his questions. "Are you a resident?" he finally asked.

"Yes, I am," Ike responded firmly, pushing the papers across the desk that showed his ownership of the property.

The clerk picked up the papers, made exact notes

about the location of the land, and then returned them to Ike.

"That about does it," the clerk said, gathering up the notes he had made. "It takes a few weeks to process your application. Meanwhile, I will look for any property we have close to where you are located."

We exchanged surprised glances. Nobody had expected it to go this easily.

I didn't want to push our luck, but I was curious about the possibility of land close to ours. I asked what the chances were of finding something nearby. The clerk opened a file drawer, searched through it for a couple minutes and then examined some papers he had extracted.

"Well," he said eventually, "there appears to be land very close to yours, but it may depend on squatters on the property." He looked at the confused expressions on our faces, then continued.

"If someone has settled on land belonging to the state, built a structure and worked the land in some way, he may lay claim to the land under a law allowing what is called adverse possession. The state will usually recognize the tenant's rights in these cases. We can talk about that more after they approve your application."

With that, he returned the papers to a file drawer and leaned forward to shake Ike's hand. "We'll be in touch, sir. I was wounded at Chattanooga," he said, glancing downward. He rolled himself away from the desk and left us to make our way outside.

We stood outside, looking at each other and wondering if it was really going to be this easy to claim 1,280 acres. After a moment, Ike pointed down the street at a saloon sign. "Celebration time," he boomed, and he led the way down the street.

————

Karras crouched in the brush, maybe fifty feet away from the little makeshift corral that McCabe had built. He could see the horse he wanted to steal, standing contentedly on the far side of the corral. It was the sorrel with the white blaze on his face. This hadn't been as easy as Karras had expected it to be. Part of the problem was that the corral was up on the plateau, about one hundred yards away from the cabin. Getting into it unobserved would have been a problem in any case. The other problem was the old codger, Boone, was doing some work over there on some kind of furniture. He kept a rifle pretty handy and glanced over frequently to check the horses. Karras could have shot him from ambush, but Diehl had made it clear there was to be no trouble near the town. He sighed and settled in to wait a little longer.

As the early afternoon sun climbed overhead, nothing seemed to change about the current situation. The woman brought some lunch to Boone, but he stayed on the job, only taking an occasional bite as he continued to build what appeared to be a bed frame. Karras took a sip from his canteen, thankful that he'd had the good sense to bring that up here with him. His food was in his saddlebags on his horse, which was tethered in the woods down below, well away from the pasture. If he got hungry enough, he thought, he might have to risk retracing his steps back down to the horse.

In mid-afternoon, his luck finally changed. The woman came out of the house to talk to Boone, and he could clearly hear the conversation from where he lay. Karras wiped the sweat away from his eyes, squinting toward the house as he listened.

"Boone," she said, "you don't have to stay here all day. They'll be home in the early evening, I think, and I don't want you to miss any pay for doing your work at the saloon." She glanced down at the bed frame. "You're almost done with this one, aren't you? You can go on home after you finish it."

Boone looked at the woman, then swept a glance around the clearing. Karras ducked down instinctively, even though he knew he was well concealed in the brush. Finally, Boone spoke. "If you're sure it's okay with you, ma'am, I'll go on when I'm done with this one. You'll want to send one of those boys out here ever' now and then. Have 'em bring a rifle and be careful. They'll need to look down yonder at the pasture and make sure the horses are all right over there in the corral." He gestured in that direction, and Karras ducked again. "They must bring 'em some water before too long." He paused and looked around doubtfully.

"It will be fine, Boone," she told him. "Ike and the others will be home soon."

Boone nodded and bent down to finish work on the bed frame.

Karras chafed while Boone took his time finishing his work. After another half hour or more, Boone put his tools down and called out to the cabin. One boy came out and helped him carry the bed frame inside. Boone reappeared, caught up his horse, which he had tethered close to the cabin, and rode away. The same boy, the younger one by the appearance of him, came back outside carrying a Winchester in the crook of his arm, and waved goodbye to Boone. He took a short stroll around the cabin, not getting close to the corral, and settled down against the side of the house. Karras eyed the Winchester warily. He could afford to wait a little longer.

Karras was dozing off despite his determination to watch for his chance. Suddenly, a slight noise roused him and he looked up to see the boy emerge from behind the cabin, carrying a large bucket of water. He had the bucket in one hand and the Winchester in the other, but he was clearly struggling with the weight of the bucket. After several more steps, he set the bucket down and walked back to the cabin, leaning the Winchester against the wall. He returned to the bucket of water, picked it up, and advanced toward the corral. Karras quietly gathered his feet under him. This was the chance he had been waiting for.

He watched as the boy approached the corral, opened the gate, and walked inside with the water bucket. The three horses inside picked up their ears and moved toward him. The boy talked to the horses soothingly, and the words helped to cover the slight amount of noise that Karras was making as he slipped quietly around to the corral gate. He pulled his gun and reversed it as he moved up behind the boy. One horse laid back his ears and whinnied, and the boy spun around. Karras leaped forward and struck him on the head with the butt of his gun, catching him and easing him to the ground as he fell.

Karras moved quickly, hoping that the woman hadn't come out of the cabin and looked in this direction. He returned his gun to the holster, grabbed the boy under his arms and dragged him out of the corral. He pulled the gate shut, then dragged the boy into the underbrush where he couldn't be seen from the cabin. He returned to his hiding place and picked up the rope he had brought, shaking out a loop as he returned to the corral. He slipped back inside and tossed the loop over the head of McCabe's sorrel, leading him out of the corral and closing it behind him.

He led the horse to as much tree cover as he could find and worked his way off the plateau, down the hillside to the west of the cabin. He risked a glance over his shoulder, and his luck was holding so far. When he reached the bottom of the hillside, he was able to move immediately into a thicker stand of trees and foliage. After about five minutes he reached his horse and mounted, tying the rope to his saddle horn. He moved to the north, toward the Diehl ranch. He wasn't really worried about leaving a trail. He wanted to be followed.

When he reached the Diehl property, he crossed the pasture and moved through the woods to find the trail he was looking for. There was a much more traveled road leading north and east toward Waco, but he didn't want that one. He wanted the narrow, winding trail with fewer travelers. That's the one that suited his purposes. When he struck upon the trail, he dismounted and made a half-hearted effort to cover his tracks. He couldn't make this too obvious. Dragging the branch across the hoof prints one more time, he stood back and surveyed his efforts. Satisfied, he re-mounted and headed north again. He had several miles to go before he reached his ambush spot. He planned to keep moving until it was dark, then he planned to set out again early. With any luck, he could reach the place by mid-morning.

———

Jeanne left the cabin and shielded her eyes against the late afternoon sun. Isaac had been outside on watch for a few hours now, and it wasn't like him not to at least stick his head inside and ask for more water, or maybe food. She didn't see him anywhere in the clearing, so she walked around the cabin to check that area. He wasn't at the gunpits, as she had come to think of the stacks of firewood overlooking the pasture. She stood behind one of the stacks, looking for him in the pasture below. When she saw no sign of him, she felt a gnawing worry start in the pit of her stomach. She shouted his name twice, but heard no answer.

"Pete!" When her older son came out of the cabin where he had finished assembling the beds, she waved her hand around the clearing, beginning to feel panic setting in. "Isaac isn't here! I don't know where he's gone!"

Pete stared for a moment, uncomprehending, then gestured toward the back of the plateau. "At the well! He's probably gone down to get water!"

Jeanne shook her head miserably. "I've looked," she said, "and I've called him. He's not here."

They circled the cabin one time, then there was a rustling noise from the direction of the corral. Pete locked eyes with his mother, then sprinted toward the corral. He found Isaac sitting up in the underbrush, holding his head with both hands. There was blood running down his face. Pete kneeled beside his brother, then Jeanne rushed past him and enveloped Isaac in a hug. Her questions poured out, one after the other. "Are you all right? Can you hear me? What happened?"

Isaac shook his head by way of reply to the last question, then grabbed his head with both hands at the fresh wave of pain produced by the motion.

Jeanne moved to his side to put an arm around him, then motioned to Pete to do the same. They lifted him slowly, then walked him back to the cabin. Jeanne eased him into the one chair they had, then grabbed a rag, and walked around behind the cabin to wet it in the water barrel. She came back inside and washed the blood from his face and head. Isaac relaxed back into the chair, then talked slowly and clearly.

Jeanne heaved a sigh of relief. "Tell us what happened when you're able," she said.

Isaac frowned in concentration, then shrugged. "I had just taken a bucket of water out to the horses. One of them laid his ears back and whinnied. I was just turning around to see what was back there, then everything blacked out."

Pete stood for a moment, then spun and ran back out to the corral. He was back in a minute or less, shouting, as he came through the door.

"Jake's horse!" he yelled. "Someone has stolen Sherman!" He raced past Jeanne and Isaac, grabbed a rifle, and started back toward the door.

Jeanne grabbed his arm to stop him. "No, Pete! You don't know who is out there, and I don't want you going out there by yourself. We will wait for your father and Jake to handle this."

Pete shouted in frustration and tried to pull away, but Jeanne held her grip tightly.

"We wait," she repeated. "They will be home soon. I need you here."

Pete shook his head and tried again to pull away, but

his mother would not relent. Finally, he nodded his head in agreement and collapsed to the floor in frustration.

———

Jeanne came running out of the cabin as we approached. Our excitement about the events at the Land Office collapsed quickly as she approached the wagon. Pete trailed behind his mother, glancing back at the cabin from time to time and carrying a rifle at his side. Jeanne clutched Ike's sleeve as he maneuvered down from the wagon.

"Isaac's hurt!" she blurted out. Then she looked at me and said, "Someone has stolen your horse."

Ike grabbed his crutch and hopped alongside her toward the cabin. I turned and swung Julia down from the wagon and hurried toward the cabin with her, glancing over toward the corral as we went.

We found Isaac lying on a blanket in one bed. He tried to push himself up to a sitting position as we came in, but Jeanne quickly kneeled and tugged him back down onto the blanket. He remained where he was, filling in the story about the attack in the corral, reaching to touch his head gingerly from time to time. When he had finished, Ike swung around, his face a thundercloud.

"Pete! Saddle up your horse and ride to town. Get the doctor to come out if you can. And see if Boone can come back out." He glanced at the rifle Pete was still carrying. "Good idea," he said. "Take that with you."

Pete dashed out the door as Jeanne slipped a pillow back under Isaac's head and did her best to make him more comfortable. When she had finished, she looked up at me. "Sherman's gone from the corral," she said. "None of the other horses are gone. I saw a few tracks leading away to the north." She pointed toward Diehl's property. "I didn't follow them," she finished. "I came inside with Isaac."

I nodded and moved outside. Ike and Julia came along with me, and we walked over to the corral. As Jeanne had said, there were a few tracks—the footprints of a man, along with Sherman's hoof prints leading away from the corral. The tracks led directly to the hill leading down to the pasture, then into the woods bordering the pasture on the west side. I followed on foot no farther than that, then returned to the corral. Ike and Julia watched me.

"You can take my horse if you want to go after him now," she offered.

I glanced toward the setting sun in the west and decided there was enough light to get started today. I began moving back toward the cabin where I still kept my knapsack and clothes. I gathered up what I needed and waited while Julia quickly put some food into a burlap bag. I glanced at Isaac, he appeared to be resting comfortably in the bed. I took my leave of Ike and Jeanne. Julia walked back to the corral with me and watched while I saddled her horse.

"I think it's a little strange they only took your horse, don't you?" she asked.

I finished bridling her horse and considered that. "Yes," I said after a moment. "If it was just a horse thief, he could have stolen the other ones too."

She followed me as I led the horse out of the corral, then put a hand on my arm as I started to mount up.

"I know you'll be careful," she said, "but I feel like I need to say it, anyway."

I bent to give her a kiss. "I'll be back before you know it," I said. Then, I began to follow the tracks leading away from the corral.

# CHAPTER 11

## MAN FROM NOWHERE

Diehl sat on his horse at the western edge of his property and watched through his binoculars as Karras made his way back across the pasture and into the trees on the other side. There were tracks clearly visible in the soft earth—two sets of hoofprints. Diehl could see them from here through the glasses. Covering tracks was not part of the plan, he reminded himself. Karras had crossed only twenty yards short of Diehl's land, leading a horse which Diehl presumed to be McCabe's. He let the binoculars hang from a strap around his neck and considered briefly the possibility of shooting McCabe from here, once McCabe followed, then dragging his body across the property line and claiming he'd only shot a trespasser. It was tempting, but he couldn't be sure that Sheriff Daniels would support him, not with the election so close. He moved his horse farther back into the trees and waited to see if McCabe would pursue.

Julia kept herself busy back at the cabin, insisting that her mother get some rest while she watched Isaac. She continued to bathe his head and neck with cool, wet cloths. He seemed drowsy, but she would feel better if she could keep him awake until the doctor arrived, so she kept talking to him, nudging him slightly when he failed to answer. On her trips out to the water barrel to moisten the cloths, she watched the pasture off in the distance. On her fourth trip, she could see someone crossing the pasture at the far end. She shaded her eyes and watched for a minute. It was one man on a horse, so she figured it must be Jake, not the horse thief. She watched until he crossed into the trees on the east side, then hurried back to her brother.

Evening shadows were lengthening across the yard in front of the cabin when Julia heard hoof beats out front. She heard her mother stir on a bed across the room. Julia went to the door of the cabin and saw three men dismounting. One was her brother Pete, and the other two were the town doctor and Boone. Jeanne came up behind her as Ike joined the men in the front. Julia stood aside as Doc Freeman hurried into the cabin, then waited with the others while he examined Isaac, shining a lantern into his eyes from time to time and asking questions. Eventually, he seemed satisfied, gave Isaac a pat on the shoulder and turned to Ike and Jeanne.

"I think he'll be fine," he told them. "Might have a headache for a couple more days. Just let him rest and get some good sleep tonight. I'll check back in a couple days."

Ike and Julia trailed after the doctor outside and saw him off. Boone joined them, having toured the plateau and checked the corral.

Ike gathered them together in the front yard, motioning to Pete to come over as well. "The way I see it," said Ike without preamble, "is that this is a good time for Diehl to try to run us off, seein' as how we're missing our best rifle shot right now. He might try to attack and take this place over."

A low murmur of agreement came from Boone, who was clearly upset that Isaac had been attacked after Boone left.

"I'll stay at that little barricade we built down yonder," said Boone, pointing at the barricade he'd built with Jake at the foot of the hill.

"You got it," said Ike. "Pete, you spell Boone from time to time and let him get some sleep. I'll be at that stack of firewood over there at the back of the house. Pete, you can take a turn at the other stack of logs over there and watch the pasture with me when you're not spellin' Boone down below. Julia," he concluded, "keep a rifle handy and watch the front of the place." He looked around the circle of faces. "What else?" he asked. "We'll have two shifts of night watch every night. I'll take the first one."

They drifted inside for dinner, but Julia stayed outside for a few minutes, walking to the back of the plateau again, staring down at the place where she had seen Jake cross. The light was fading tonight, but she decided that in the next couple days she would take the road down to the place where Jake might have emerged from the trees over there to the east. She wanted to have some idea of what direction he had taken. She couldn't shake the feeling that he was headed into some kind of trap. A shout from the cabin told her that dinner was ready. She

took one more look across the pasture, then went inside
to join the family.

———

Karras pushed the pace as he rode the trail toward Waco.
He intended to stop well short of there, but he had to
reach the ambush point tonight. He couldn't have
McCabe overtaking him before he reached that spot. The
sorrel horse he had stolen was following willingly enough
—still, McCabe was probably making better speed than
he was. No telling how much head start he'd gotten. He
glanced around. The fading light was going to make it
harder to get his bearings. He swore under his breath and
kept urging his horse forward.

He rounded several more bends in the trail, finally
admitting to himself that he would have to stop for the
night if he didn't come across the place he was looking
for soon. He couldn't afford to pass it up in the dark. His
hopes picked up as the trail bent quickly to the right,
then straightened out in front of him. A pile of logs and
brush off to the left caught his attention. He pulled the
horses over, dismounted, and walked up to the logs. This
was the place. He pulled the horses back into the woods
and built a small cooking fire behind the pile of logs.
When he had eaten, he carried his rifle to the logs and
sighted through a chink between them. He had an excellent field of fire on the trail, and when it was fully light
tomorrow, he should have no trouble. When it was dark,
he spread out his blankets and turned in. He would be up
early in the morning, waiting for his chance.

———

I emerged from the woods and struck the trail, following the hoofprints in front of me. It seemed pretty clear that he had taken the trail north and east. I followed along easily, remembering to scan the area in front of me for anybody who might have bushwhacking in mind. I came to a fork in the road, with one fork looking wider and more traveled, branching off in a little more easterly direction. The one leading to the north and west was much narrower, and appeared to be more winding. There was only one recent set of tracks leading that way, but they looked like the tracks I had been following. I got down and inspected them more closely. When I stood, I was pretty sure I needed the branch to the left. It looked like someone had tried to cover the tracks a little and had done a poor job of it. I stared skeptically down the trail. This seemed a little too good to be true.

Finally, I re-mounted and started up the left branch of the trail. I was moving more slowly now, leerier of sharp bends in the trail and mindful of the failing light. Once in a while, I got down and checked the tracks again, and the droppings left by the horses. I estimated he was an hour or two ahead of me. I pushed on until I couldn't see over fifty yards in front of me. I didn't want him to gain time on me, but I figured he wouldn't be traveling in the dark, either. I pulled over and rubbed down Julia's horse, then made a little dinner with the food Julia had packed for me. I didn't start a fire. No sense in giving away my location.

I was awake before sunrise and had to wait for a little more light before beginning. I had eaten, saddled the horse and been ready to go for almost a half hour before the early morning sunlight filtered through the post oak trees. I held on for another twenty minutes to make sure I could see well enough to spot the tracks and scan the woods in front of me. Finally, I swung into the saddle and struck the trail, leaning over slightly, both to read the trail and to present a smaller target. Julia's words about how curious it was that only one horse had been stolen were echoing in my mind this morning.

The trail was a little older this morning, I could see that right away. The droppings were no longer fresh, and the tracks weren't as distinct. They were definitely the same tracks, but I concluded he had ridden farther last night than I had before stopping. There didn't seem to be any danger of losing the trail this morning, as they were still the only ones on this trail. I pushed ahead a little faster, anyway. I was eager to find the spot where he had started out again this morning. I didn't want him disposing of Sherman before I caught up to him.

My mind went back to the events of the evening before. I wondered if this might be a ploy to get me away from the ranch. I could only hope that Ike and Boone would step up their watchfulness and not be caught by surprise if anyone attacked the ranch. I had traveled for close to an hour, and it still appeared to be a trail left last night. I wondered how far he would have gone after dark, if at all. I came around a bend in the trail and was surprised to see a straightaway stretch in front of me. It was the first I had seen since taking this left fork trail last night.

I bent over a little to check some droppings on the trail—they weren't fresh. I straightened up a bit to check the scene in front of me. A slight movement caught my eye, and then the brief reflection of sunlight on metal shone behind a pile of logs. Ambush! My reflexes from my army days were thankfully still with me. I reached for the Spencer and kicked my feet out of the stirrups as I twisted to the side. Then I felt a tremendous blow strike me on my head, and the world went dark.

Karras rose from his position and walked around the log barricade where he had been waiting. This had been a little harder than he thought—he'd never dry-gulched a man before. He stepped out onto the trail, already feeling a little nervous about being found out here by somebody passing by. He glanced over his shoulder and took a couple tentative steps toward McCabe. He knew he'd hit the man in the head because he'd seen McCabe's head snap back after the shot. He was lying still on the trail, blood coming from the side of his head. Karras turned and untied McCabe's sorrel and slapped the horse on the rump. He gathered up the reins to his horse, mounted, and struck the trail to the north. He would take a round-about route home. He didn't want to hang around here anymore.

He glanced back one more time before a bend in the trail that would take him out of sight. McCabe's sorrel horse had stopped and was nuzzling the body on the road. The other horse was cropping grass at the side of the trail. Too bad about leaving the horses. He could have sold them for good money. But he didn't need anybody hanging him as a horse thief. He needed some distance from this shooting, and he needed it now. He put the spurs to his horse and disappeared around the bend in the trail.

———

I awoke to find myself lying awkwardly on my side in the middle of a trail. I heard a snuffling noise and realized something was sniffing at my face. I turned my head slightly and was rewarded with a thunderclap of pain exploding in my head. I moaned and rolled onto my back, staring up at a blue sky and sun about halfway overhead. I turned my head slightly and saw a sorrel horse with a white blaze on his face nuzzling me. I gathered my strength and turned onto my side, then pushed myself to a sitting position. The pain was making me feel nause-ated. I stared dumbly at a pool of blood soaking into the dust of the trail, then put a hand to the side of my head. It was my blood.

I stayed in the sitting position and allowed the nausea to pass. I concentrated, trying to remember what had put me in this position. I had a vague memory of riding down this trail, turning a corner, then feeling something strike my head. But after that...I couldn't remember anything. Nothing at all. I stood up, moving very slowly, and went through my pockets. I found some money in one pocket, but nothing else. No papers. I realize I couldn't even remember my name or where I'd come from. I walked slowly over to the saddled horse, a smaller dun-colored mare. I searched through the saddlebags. There was some food and a little more money, along with some ammuni-tion for the Colt on my hip and the Spencer carbine I saw laying in the middle of the trail. I picked it up and returned it to the scabbard on the saddle.

The gelding sorrel horse had followed me to the side of the trail, then cropped some grass. I noticed that the female followed the gelding when he moved. Apparently, they knew each other. Did I have two horses? Where was I going with them? I pulled some food from the saddle-bags and took the canteen off the saddle horn. I perched on a rock and ate a bit, then drank some water, feeling a little stronger afterward. The pain in my head was still intense, but no longer crippling. I pondered what to do next. I had no idea who I was or where I had been headed.

An idea occurred to me, and I walked over to examine the brands on the horses. The little mare had a rocking *H* brand on it. The sorrel had a box *M* brand. Neither meant anything to me. I sighed with frustration and walked back out to the middle of the trail, looking north and south. I had no idea which way was home. After a while, I went over and switched the saddle and bridle from the mare to the gelding sorrel horse. He looked bigger and stronger, and seemed more familiar with me. I took the rope hanging from my saddle and tied the mare to the saddle horn on the sorrel. Then I mounted up and stared one more time, north and south. Finally, I turned the sorrel to the north and started down the trail.

I saw tracks in front of me as I traveled north. It was one rider. I couldn't tell much more. The heat from the midday sun told me I was probably in the south somewhere. There didn't seem to be any other clues to be found. I estimated it was around noon when I swung down and had a little more to eat. The dizziness and pain in my head were easing a little further, but I still had no memory of anything beyond this morning. After another hour on the trail, I saw the tracks in front of me swing off to the east. I pulled up and looked where the tracks were leading. It seemed to be a very faint trail into some thick underbrush. I studied it for a minute, then decided I was better off continuing on the trail I was currently following.

By mid-afternoon, I was fighting the urge to doze off in the saddle. I was anxious to get to the next town, hoping it would jog my memory, or at the least, maybe I could find a doctor to look at the wound. I spotted a wooden signpost stuck into the ground up ahead. I pulled up, dismounted, and brushed the dirt and mud off the sign. An arrow pointed upward with the word *Waco*. Well, at least I knew I was in Texas. It didn't say how far it was to Waco, so I re-mounted and kept going.

By the time the sun was well down in the sky, I had to admit to myself that I would not reach Waco before dark. The surrounding terrain was changing a bit, as the tree line was slowly giving way to rolling fields of grass. I made camp at the edge of the forest, keeping the horses back in the trees a bit and putting out my bedroll back off the trail. I had to assume I still had enemies out there, even if I seemed to be alone on this road.

It was late afternoon or early evening the next day when the trail widened, and I could see the buildings of a town in front of me. Another half hour's ride and I was walking the horses down the street of what I assumed to be Waco. A couple signs on the storefronts confirmed I was right. I saw a livery stable and led the horses in. An older man emerged and showed me where I could tether the horses. He glanced at the blood on the side of my head.

"That's a nasty-looking wound, bud," he said, not unsympathetically. "What happened to you?"

I could only shrug.

"Don't want to say," he concluded. "That's okay." He took my money, studied me for a moment, then pointed across the street. "Hotel right there if you need it, Bud."

I turned and walked to the street. I paused there, looking up and down in both directions—searching for a sign, a building, a person or anything else that might jog my memory. There was nothing. I crossed the street to the hotel, walked in and up to the desk to sign in. The clerk pushed a book across the desk at me.

"What's your name?" he asked. I stared at him for a moment.

"Bud," I said finally.

# CHAPTER 12

## ALONE

I stirred my coffee absently and waited for the server to bring my eggs. She had looked at the side of my head from time to time while taking the order, and I couldn't blame her. There was a jagged furrow across the left side of my head. A nasty bruise was forming over the temple. I had cleaned it again as best I could, but decided I should look for a doctor first thing this morning. When my breakfast came, I stopped the girl as she turned to go.

"Miss?" She turned back. "Is there a doctor in town?"

She glanced at the wound again, then broke into the briefest of smiles. She pointed across the street and down maybe a block. "Dr. Abrams," she said. "He's my uncle."

———

The doctor was seeing a patient out as I entered. He looked at me and let out a low whistle.

"Bullet wound," he said. It wasn't a question.

"I think so," was my only answer.

He searched my face for a moment. "You don't remember, do you?"

I shook my head slowly.

"Come on back," he said, steering me into a side room.

He sat me down on the table and looked at the wound, making a few clucking noises as he did so. Then he had me tilt my head over, and he poured something on it that stung like crazy. I could have used a little warning, I thought. I made a slight moaning noise as he finished pouring, then he wound a cloth around my head.

Next, he sat me in the bright light pouring through the window and watched my eyes as he moved some things around in front of me. He looked into my eyes a while longer, then began asking me some questions. As long as the questions weren't anything about my past, I could answer. Finally, he sat back and looked at me.

"Tell me what happened, as best you can remember," he said.

"There's not much to tell," I responded. "I rode around a bend in the trail coming up somewhere south of here a couple days ago and felt a tremendous blow to my head. I woke up, probably a couple hours later, and couldn't remember anything else from the past. I don't even know my name."

He waved at me to join him in his office, then sat down in a chair next to me. "We call what you've got amnesia," he said. "I mean, the part about losing your memory. Sometimes, it does seem to happen when you've had a blow to your head. You'll probably remember some things pretty soon. Maybe a few days. It might have to do with swelling from the gunshot...I don't know. It might help to be around people or places you know, but I guess you don't have that choice. You're away from home and you don't know where you live." He paused and stared at the floor for a minute. I leaned back in the chair and waited.

"What would you do if you were me?" I asked.

He thought for a moment. "I would probably stay around here for a few days," he said. "You don't know which way to go to get home or find people you know. If you leave here, you might get farther away from them. If you stay here, maybe somebody will find you. Or you might just start to remember, soon."

I picked up my hat and moved to the door.

"There's one more thing," he said.

I turned to look at him.

"There's somebody in town who had something similar happen a few years ago. I don't guess he would mind me telling you. Maybe you could talk to him."

I waited. He pointed down the street.

"Jed, over at the livery stable. He lost his memory for a week or two, several years back. Maybe he can tell you a little more about it."

I pulled the door shut and stood in the morning sunlight, trying to decide the best thing to do. I had enough money to stay here for a while. Maybe I could even make a few bucks at the livery stable and find out what else I could learn about this condition. I started to put my hat on, thought better of it, and walked down to the livery stable.

————

"He's dead. I done it myself. Saw the bullet hit him in the head. Saw him go down. Lots of blood on the trail. Straight-up shootin'. Done." Karras squirmed a little under Diehl's relentless stare, but stuck to his story.

Diehl picked up a pocketknife laying on the desk and tossed it up and down. "Where did this happen?"

Karras pointed out the window, vaguely motioning to the north. "I got him to follow me on the trail up toward Waco. The old trail on the left that nobody uses anymore. He followed me till it was dark the first night. Then I waited for him around a bend the next mornin'." Karras stopped, clearly thinking the conversation was complete.

Diehl continued to toss the knife up and down. "And then?"

Karras paused, halfway to sitting down in a chair at the side of the room. He stood back up and stammered a few words. He hadn't really rehearsed the story this far.

"And then," he continued, "I braced him right there in the road. Asked him why he was follerin' me around. Told him to get off his horse and tell me why."

Diehl put down the pocketknife and pounced. "So, you drew on him and shot him in the head? Why didn't you aim for the chest? Who aims for the head in a gunfight?"

Karras, clearly stumped, stared at the ground for a moment, then improvised. "Well, first, I shot him in the chest and knocked him down. But he was still tryin' to get his gun up on me, so then I shot him in the head. Knocked him right down in the road. He's dead. Didn't move once." He lifted his eyes to look at Diehl, still fidgeting and clearly uncomfortable. Diehl decided to let it go for now.

"Okay," he said, spilling a few gold coins on the desk.

Karras walked over and reached to pick up the coins. Diehl reached out, grabbed his wrist, and pinned it to the table. Karras grimaced with pain. "I better not hear he's still alive," Diehl said. "That would be a problem. I like to deal with problems right away."

Karras flinched, withdrew his hand and put the coins in his pocket. "He's dead," he repeated, and left the room.

Diehl stood and walked to the window, watching Karras walk to the bunkhouse. He didn't believe the straight-up shooting story for a minute, but that didn't matter if the job got done and he had done it far enough out of town. He would have to keep his ear to the ground on this one. He didn't know any other way to check it out besides riding up that trail, which was out of the question. If Karras hadn't gotten it done, well, Al Vincent was coming to town and Karras had outlived his usefulness.

———

I stood in the street outside the livery stable and counted the money in my pocket. I would not sleep in the livery stable, that was for sure. I had enough money to stay at the hotel for a couple weeks and have meals at the café, but I didn't feel like spending everything I had. Maybe I could do some work at the livery stable, learn what I could about this memory loss from Jed, or whatever his name was, and still have a few dollars in my pocket. I looked up to see Jed watching me over a rail fence at the stable. I walked on in.

"Hey, Bud." He walked over and began tossing a few bales of hay into a feed rack. "What's on your mind?" I went over and helped him toss a few more bales.

"I was wondering," I began, "if I could do a little work

for you for a week. I could feed and walk the horses, clean out a few stalls, do whatever you need."

Jed stopped and leaned against a rail. "You say for a week?"

I nodded.

He shrugged. "I guess I could pay you two dollars a day. That all right?"

It covered the hotel cost, so I agreed. He turned, picked up a shovel, and handed it to me.

"You know what to do with this, I'm thinking." I grinned and headed for the first stall. "By the way," he said, "what's your name?"

I stopped and looked back at him. "Bud will do," I said.

He looked at me shrewdly, then glanced at the bandage wrapped around my head. "You don't know what it is, do you?" I shook my head and started shoveling out the stall.

When lunch rolled around, I walked down to the general store and bought a few things. I came back to find Jed perched on a hay bale, finishing up a bowl of beef and beans. He waved to the spot next to him. "Lost my memory for a while one time," he said. I glanced over at him.

"That's what the doc told me."

He nodded and stared out at the street. "Got in a fight with a guy at a ranch where I worked a little south of here. Was gettin' the better of him, I was. Then he grabbed a board and went upside my head to finish things off." He touched a spot near his left temple. "I drifted up here, started remembering things after about a week. Got this livery stable going and stayed here. Near onto twenty years ago, now."

"Anything you did that helped you remember?" I asked.

He shook his head. "Nah, just started comin' back, a little at a time."

He pointed at my gun belt, which I had hung over a post when I started working. "You any good with that thing?" he asked.

I paused. "I don't really know."

"Well, I figure you've got an enemy or two," he said. "You might want to find out if you're any good an' practice with it." That sounded familiar to me, but I couldn't place a voice or a face saying that before. Jed watched me for a minute. "I could teach you some about using it," he said.

I looked over in surprise. "You good with a six-shooter?"

He shrugged. "I'm not all that good, but I know how to use it. The rest is reflexes. Mine aren't that great." He leaned over and spit on the ground. "And at my age, they ain't gettin' no better, neither."

I chuckled and finished up my lunch.

"Do you feel natural and comfortable puttin' it on?" he asked.

I thought for a second. "A little. It feels more normal when I pick up the Spencer."

He considered that for a minute. "That probly means you ain't from around here, if you're not comfortable with the six guns. Maybe from back east somewhere. Around here, folks mostly defend themselves with pistols."

That made sense to me. An image flashed through my mind for a second of a greener, hillier place, thick with trees. Then, the image faded. I looked up to see Jed staring at me.

"Rememberin' something?" he asked.

I shrugged. "Maybe just for a second."

He nodded. "That's how it started for me." He picked up my gun belt from the post and brought it over. "Put it on and show me what you got."

I took it from him and strapped it on.

"Hold on," he said. He took the gun out of the holster, shook the bullets out into his hand, then gave it back. "Okay, now."

I drew the gun and dropped it back into the holster several times while he watched critically.

"Not bad," he said. "You're fast pulling it out of the holster. Need to give it a little more lift before you start forward with it. Worst thing is to get it caught on the top of the holster. Give it a little more room at the top of the draw."

Surprised at the knowledge he was showing about this, I took his advice and practiced again and again with the draw until he was satisfied.

"Okay," he said. "Show me how you draw and fire."

I pulled the pistol several times, giving a little more clearance over the holster before I started forward, then eared it back and pulled the trigger.

He watched me, then shook his head. "You got to stop moving afore you fire that thing. Can't hit nothin' you want to hit if the gun's still movin'. Take a little bit longer, bring it to a stop, then fire and hit what you're aiming at."

I practiced what he'd told me until he pronounced himself satisfied. He took the gun, returned the bullets to the chamber, then handed it back to me. "When we're done workin' we can go out of town a little way and practice it for real."

After we were done for the day at the stable, he proved as good as his word. We rode out of town a couple miles, then he set up empty beer bottles on a log and told me to fire away. When I missed, he would shake his head impatiently.

"Steady it down first, hit what you're aimin' at."

Again, those words sounded so familiar, but there was no face to go with the words. I concentrated on Jed's advice, firing again and again until the bottles shattered on nearly every try. Finally, he pronounced himself satisfied, and we mounted up to go back to town.

"If I was you," he said seriously, "I'd come out here and practice every night."

Sitting in the café a little later on, I had to admit that Jed was right. I must have enemies out there, or at least one. Somebody had come within about an inch of killing me with that headshot. Me not knowing who it was put me in a pretty dangerous position. What if they had followed me and were looking to finish the job? I resolved to go out and practice every night, as Jed had told me. I glanced around the room. Nobody had looked familiar to me since I had arrived in town, but that really meant nothing.

Out in the kitchen, I could see the husband and wife, owners of the café, cooking on an old wooden stove. A boy came in carrying an armful of firewood. The husband opened the door on the stove, and they tossed in a few logs. I watched the flames leap up, and an image popped into my head. There was a cabin sitting on a green hillside. Flames were leaping up, burning down the cabin. I was standing helplessly, watching the cabin burn down.

"Sir, are you okay?" The woman was standing by my table, touching me on the shoulder. "Are you okay?" she repeated. I shook my head for a moment, then waved her off.

"I'm fine," I said. I paid the bill and walked outside, then turned and headed for the saloon. Maybe a drink was what I needed.

———

Al Vincent surveyed the cards he was holding and helped himself to another shot of whiskey. He motioned to the boy to leave the bottle on the table. He looked at his hand again, liked what he saw, and raised the bet. This would be his last hand for tonight, he decided. He was up for the night and didn't like to push his luck. When the betting was done, he showed a full house against two pair. He swept up his winnings and moved over to another table, where the four men he had hired for this job were drinking but staying out of trouble, just like he'd ordered. Another two days of riding after this stopover in Waco and they would be ready to get the job done and go home.

Vincent deposited his whiskey bottle on the table and took a seat, looking around the table. He hadn't bothered to learn any names.

"Everybody squared away? We know what we're doing?"

A man on his left, who seemed to be the loudest one, snorted. "We chase a few drifters from Kentucky off a few acres. Easy."

Vincent stared at him, concealing his thoughts. He'd known a few guys from Kentucky who carried their rifles like they'd been born with them. Maybe this was easy and maybe it wasn't. He decided to hang back a little on this job and let these guys take their chances. If it was easy, fine. If not...these guys could find out.

"Right," he said. "We'll find out how easy."

He lifted the whiskey bottle again and found, to his surprise and irritation, it was empty. He picked it up and moved back to the bar.

He ordered one more shot and glanced down the bar. He saw a tall, dark-haired man with a bandage wrapped around his head, drinking beer. He hadn't seen the man before, which wasn't a surprise down here in Waco, but the bandage caught his attention. He stopped the bartender when he passed by and pointed.

"What's his story?"

The bartender looked down at the man with the bandage, picked up the empty whiskey bottle and wiped down the bar.

"Just been here a couple days," he said. "Folks think maybe he got bushwhacked somewhere around here. Doesn't seem to know his name or remember anything about himself. That's what I hear, anyway." Vincent tossed down the last whiskey for the night and turned away. He hated bushwhackers.

# CHAPTER 13

## DREAMS AND MEMORIES

It had been two days since Jake had left to follow the horse thief, Julia reflected as she staked out the corners of a vegetable garden. She had located the garden at the foot of the plateau, near the well. Watering would be a lot easier down here, and she had planned it so there would be morning sun and afternoon shade. She wasn't sure what she could still plant in the late spring, but she would ask around. She straightened up from her task to watch her mother, who had come down to help. With Isaac improving and doing some light work again, Jeanne had brightened up as well. Julia believed she could see her mother warming to the idea of creating a home for her family in their new surroundings.

Julia leaned on her shovel and stared absently at the far end of the pasture, where she had last seen Jake when he had gone after the horse thief. Two days wasn't a long time, but it wasn't unreasonable to think he could have been home by now. She had wanted to ride down the road for a bit and look for any signs of where he might have gone, but Ike was insistent she stay near the cabin and help guard against any invasions of their land. She shielded her eyes and speculated on how much time she would need to check the trail for clues.

"Two days isn't a terribly long time." Julia jumped slightly before she realized that Jeanne had come alongside her. She picked up the shovel and started to dig, but Jeanne stopped her with a hand on her arm. "Ike is going into town in a little while to meet Boone and pick up some supplies. I'm sure you could borrow Pete's horse and look around a little if you want to."

Julia straightened up and looked at her mother in surprise. This was a side of her mother she hadn't seen before. "Dad told me I need to stay here with you," she pointed out.

Jeanne shrugged. "The boys and I can keep an eye out. Go if you want to."

After Ike had gone to town, she mounted up on Pete's horse and struck the trail north. It was pretty evident where tracks led from the Diehl property onto the trail. She stopped and studied the tracks for a few minutes. There was a set of two horses, then a third set of tracks with just one horse. She felt certain they were the tracks of the horse thief, followed by Jake. As the tracks merged onto the trail and moved north, there were too many tracks on the trail for her to follow Jake's path. Discouraged, she pulled up. She followed the trail north a little farther, looking for any sign of someone leaving the trail. It was all she had to work with.

She rode for about ten minutes, scanning the brush at the sides of the trail for any sign of someone pulling off into the woods. She figured she had about two hours before Ike returned, and she was determined to find whatever she could. Her patience was rewarded after another ten minutes. The trail forked. Almost all the traffic had gone to the right—it was well traveled. The fork to the left, though, had only a few sets of tracks. She moved to the left and dismounted. Studying the tracks, she found only three sets, and she felt sure they matched the ones she had seen leaving the Diehl property.

Following these tracks became a lot easier, and she urged Pete's horse into a trot as she worked her way down the trail. The biggest problem now was time. She had promised Jeanne she wouldn't be gone for more than an hour, and she was going to have to turn around soon in order to hold to that promise. She rode until she saw a single set of tracks pull off the trail and into the trees. Dismounting and following on foot, she found where Jake had apparently made camp the first night. She returned to the trail and glanced in frustration to the north. No telling how far that trail led, and she had to get home. She promised herself that if Jake wasn't home in a couple more days, she would follow that trail until she found him.

———

Boone hauled the last of the crates of beer into the back of the saloon. He promised himself he would give up this bending and hauling and lifting before too many more years went by. He checked the clock over the bar and saw that it would be another twenty minutes before Ike would join him. He pulled a mop and bucket out of the back closet, talking to himself about it under his breath. He began mopping, reflecting on the fact that Jake had ridden off two days ago. He knew that Jake could take care of himself in any kind of fair fight, but nothing said the fights would always be fair.

He worked his way toward the front of the saloon, stopping when a shadow cast through the batwing doors appeared in front of him. He glanced up, taking in first the heavy bandaging wrapped around the leg of a very dusty pair of pants. He followed the glance on up, seeing that it was Bates, one of Diehl's thugs, still nursing the gunshot wound that Jake had given him.

"Little too old to be moppin', ain't you, old-timer?" Bates's lips were curled in a sneer.

Boone ignored him and continued to mop. Bates reached out as if to grab his arm, and Boone's grip tightened around the mop handle. Bates seemed to reconsider and pulled his hand back.

"Seen your buddy McCabe lately?" Bates clearly relished the question.

Boone paused. "He's around," he said, then went back to mopping.

"Not what I hear," Bates chortled. "Kinda hard to get elected sheriff if'n you're not around no more."

Boone went back to ignoring him, and Bates noticed he was getting some threatening looks from behind the bar. That bartender/owner had a shotgun, he reminded himself. He ordered a beer, slammed it down, and limped out.

Boone finished mopping, checked the clock one more time, then put the mop and bucket away. He ordered a pitcher of beer and took a seat at a table, waiting for Ike. What Bates had said was a little troubling, he had to admit. Bates hinted that he knew Jake wouldn't be coming back. Maybe he knew something, maybe he didn't. In any case, he was right about the election for sheriff. That was coming up in just about a week. If Jake hadn't made an appearance by then, Daniels would be elected again. That was unthinkable.

Another shadow cast itself over the table, but Ike's cheerful, boisterous words accompanied this one. "Got some beer already. Good man."

Boone grinned and filled a glass, shoving it across the table at Ike.

"Checked at the courthouse," Ike announced. "No word yet on that land grant, but I'm hopeful. Mighty hopeful." He finished the glass with one long, mighty pull and reached for the pitcher. "What's wrong with you, Boone? You look mighty serious."

Boone shook off the somber mood he was in and hoisted his glass. The Hawkins family had enough trouble with Diehl already. "No problem," he announced. "Let's polish this off and get us some supplies."

———

The dreams started on the second night after I came to Waco. I was in a uniform, marching through trees, hearing bullets zinging all around me. Sometimes, a cannon ball exploded in front of me, tossing men out of the way like rag dolls. And always, there were fires. Horrible fires raging out of control in the underbrush, with men trapped under tree trunks and tree limbs, or wounded so badly they weren't able to crawl away from the fire. They called out for help, but I couldn't help them. I had to keep marching until they let us drop and take cover behind logs and brush. The fires kept coming closer, but I didn't dare raise my head and run...I yelled when the fire got close.

There was pounding on the wall from the room next door. I got up and splashed my face down with water from the bowl they had set out for me. I didn't feel like sleeping anymore, so I got up and walked around town until daylight.

Jed watched me coming into the stable that morning, noting my bleary eyes. "Bad night?" he asked.

I began tossing some hay into the racks. "I was in the war, that's for sure," I said.

He looked at me quizzically.

"Dreams," I explained.

He nodded. "Anything that helped you remember who you are or where you're from?"

I thought for a moment. "Well," I said, "I was wearing a blue uniform, so I guess I fought for the union." Jed winced and glanced around.

"You probably don't want to say that too loud around here," he advised me.

"Don't worry," I said, tossing a little more hay, "I don't want to talk about it anymore at all."

The next night I had another dream about the war, but it wasn't as horrible as the one the night before. I sat up for maybe a half hour and laid back down to sleep. This time, I saw the little cabin in the green hills, on fire like before, but there was a body lying in the yard in front of the cabin. In my dream, I turned the body over, but I couldn't recognize the face. Then, I saw myself burying the man in front of the cabin. After I buried the man, I got on my horse and rode down a trail to another cabin. There was a girl at the cabin—a beautiful dark-haired girl. We sat and talked outside the cabin, but I didn't know her name. When I woke up the next morning, her face was still clear in my mind. I just didn't know her name.

Jed watched me as I came in to work the next morning. "Well?" he asked.

I walked over and brushed one of the horses I had brought in with me. "There's a girl," I said.

Jed broke into a big grin. "There always is," he told me. "Did you know her name?"

I shook my head in frustration. "I would know that face if I see it again," I said, "but I don't know her name."

Jed patted me on the shoulder. "I remembered faces first, too. The names will start to come to you."

After I'd finished at the stables for the day, Jed rode out to watch me practice my shooting. He watched without comment while I broke six bottles out of six with the Colt. I picked up the Spencer and fired several rounds, hitting what I was aiming at pretty easily.

"Yep," he observed, "you're pretty handy with that thing."

He held out his hands, and I handed him the rifle. "It's pretty old, too. You were using this before the war." He handed it back. "Green and hilly, where you was..." He shook his head. "Could be a lot of places. North of here in Arkansas, Missouri, Tennessee, Kentucky or North Carolina. None of that rings a bell?"

I shook my head. We mounted up and rode back to town.

---

Vincent led his band of four into town in Fredericksburg. He always liked to get a feel for the town before going to see the man who had hired him. Knowing things about the town and how it operated had served him well before, when he'd found himself in a tight spot. He led the way up to the bar and ordered whiskey, noting in the reflection of a mirror that there was a shotgun on a shelf below the bar. He picked up his shot glass and turned, surveying the room. There was an old man pushing a mop who seemed to take a little extra notice of him. Vincent returned the stare, and the old man went back to mopping.

The doors pushed open, and a man came in wearing a sheriff's badge. He stopped and looked at the five men standing at the bar, then took a longer look at Vincent's two tied-down guns. He turned and walked over, stopping in front of Vincent.

"I'm the sheriff," he announced loudly. "Sheriff Daniels. Who are you?"

Vincent reached behind him and set the whiskey glass on the bar. He took his time searching in his pockets for a cigar and a match. He slowly lit the cigar and puffed the smoke into Daniel's face.

"Vincent. Al Vincent's my name." He blew another smoke ring at the sheriff.

Daniels took a half-step back and the name recognition registered on his face. He stood indecisively for a moment. "What's your business in town?"

Vincent turned and ordered another whiskey. Taking his time, he turned to face Daniels again. "That," he said, "would be my business."

Daniels held his ground for only a moment, then turned and walked out, mustering as much dignity as possible. He could hear a few snickers from the five men at the bar behind him. He reached the sidewalk outside, livid with anger but unsure what to do about it. His gut told him that Diehl had hired these men to reclaim the old Richardson property. His job depended on Diehl, that much he knew. He regained his composure. He would have to go out and talk to Diehl about this. The election was only a week away.

Back inside the bar, Vincent listened to the scraps of conversation he could overhear. A few questions to the bartender produced only a few one-word answers. Finally, as a last resort, he bought a couple drinks for two down-at-the-heels cowboys hanging around at one table. He found out that Diehl pretty much ran the town, and the sheriff, Daniels, belonged to Diehl. There was an election for sheriff coming up in a week. Armed with that information, he waved at his men, and they rode out to the Diehl ranch.

———

Diehl sat rather stiffly behind his desk, growing uncomfortable with the way Vincent was probing him for information. The questions centered on the family he wanted to chase off the land and the other man, McCabe, who was living on the property. He told Vincent what he knew—the family was from the hills of Kentucky, and the old man had only one leg. Simple thing to do, he told Vincent. It was just that he didn't have anybody else available to do the job right now. He admitted that the man McCabe had been a pretty salty character, but emphasized that McCabe wasn't in the picture anymore. When Vincent pressed for more, he refused to answer. He regretted that he had already paid Vincent half his fee.

When Diehl refused to provide any more information

about McCabe, Vincent shrugged, stood up and began walking out of the room.

"Where you going?" Diehl's tone couldn't hide his anger.

Vincent turned, walked back, and towered over him. "Home," he answered simply. "You don't give me enough information, I don't work."

Diehl struggled to his feet. "I've already paid you half your money," he growled.

Vincent's hand hung lazily on his gun belt. "This is up to you," he said in a disturbingly quiet voice.

Diehl backed away and stared out the window for a moment before answering. "McCabe's dead," he said finally. "One of my men braced and killed him a little north of here. On the road between here and Waco. That answer your question?"

Vincent nodded and turned to go, then remembered the tall, dark-haired man with the bandage around his head at the saloon in Waco. He stopped and glanced over his shoulder.

"What did this man McCabe look like?" he asked.

Diehl shrugged. "Tall, dark hair, maybe thirty. Wore one Colt, moved pretty good. Good fighter," he admitted grudgingly.

Vincent searched his pocket for a cigar, then for a match. Diehl hated the smell of cigar smoke in his library but said nothing. Vincent placed the cigar between his teeth, struck the match, and lit the cigar. Diehl waited impatiently.

"This man McCabe," Vincent said, "he might not be dead."

———

Diehl sat in his favorite cowhide-covered chair and watched Karras squirm. He had already decided that Karras was totally expendable but that didn't mean he couldn't get what he needed from him before he paid Vincent for another killing. Besides, he needed to be careful about how much Vincent knew about his business. That man was dangerous. This man, he thought, watching Karras, was a weasel.

"Tell me again," he told Karras, "how you killed McCabe."

It reminded Karras of a cat he'd had when he was a kid. That cat would lie down near a hole in the barn wall where the mice would come and go. That was a patient cat. He would wait, silent as death, until a mouse appeared, and then he would pounce. Unfortunately, in this situation, Karras was uncomfortably aware that he was the mouse. He decided it was time to tell some truth, but not all.

"I shot him in a fair, stand-up fight," he insisted. "I didn't go and check him to make sure he was dead. I thought I heard somebody coming, and I got out of there." He glanced at the revolver on the desk next to Diehl's right hand.

Diehl stared at him absently, turning over a couple possibilities in his mind. Using the revolver was one choice, but he preferred to get other people to do those things.

"Go find this man in Waco, the one with the bandage wrapped around his head. If it's McCabe, kill him. This time, bring me proof he's dead."

Karras briefly considered asking what kind of proof Diehl needed but decided against it. Best not to rile him up any further right now. He nodded and stood up.

"You have four days," Diehl told him. "Otherwise, Al Vincent will come looking for you."

Karras stood and half-walked, half-trotted out of the room. Diehl watched him go. With any luck, he thought, McCabe and Karras would kill each other. Otherwise, Vincent was going to cost him more money than he'd originally planned on.

# Chapter 14

## Range War

Vincent stayed mounted back in the trees where he thought he could be unobserved. Diehl was pressing him to mount the attack and drive the settlers off the property. Vincent was pretty sure the urgency had to do with the upcoming election for sheriff, but that really wasn't his problem. He was getting paid to get these people off the land, and although he had no scruples about how he went about that, he took a certain pride in getting things done once he had taken money to do them. He surveyed the bottom of a plateau-like structure at the back of the property. He swung the binoculars to look at the trail leading up to the top of the plateau, unaware that the movement of the glasses had resulted in a bit of glare off the lenses.

He slowly moved the line of sight across the bottom of the plateau, noting the water well and the beginnings of a garden. The near side of the plateau also showed signs of a faint trail leading up to the table-like structure above. Finally, he focused on what he could see at the top. There were two stacks of firewood at the edge that he suspected might also serve as defensive positions. He would tell his men about those firewood stacks, and he didn't plan to put himself anywhere near the line of fire. He didn't plan to put himself in harm's way at all. It's not that he minded a stand-up gun fight. There were just likely to be too many stray bullets flying around in this operation, too much chance for the unexpected. Getting killed by accident was something he let other people do.

He considered what he had learned this morning and thought about how to form up the attack on the property. This morning he had taken the road past the entrance to the place. Normally, he didn't like the idea of making a frontal attack, but he was pretty sure that was the way to do it in this case. The settlers' house was structured to guard against an invasion from Diehl's property. As he understood it, this man McCabe had already driven off a couple cowboys trying to bring in some cattle from that direction. It was pretty natural to put their best firepower behind those firewood stacks, facing Diehl's property, ready to drive off any intruders. Vincent didn't plan to disappoint them—he would have a couple guys out there in the woods, trading some shots with them. That wouldn't be the focus of the attack, though.

His morning ride had convinced him that they could attack the cabin from the front. A couple men could stay concealed until they came within about fifty yards of the cabin. There was a narrow trail leading in from the road, well concealed by a thick stand of burr oak trees until it finally curved around and opened up into the small clearing in the front. Vincent had seen a hole in the front wall of the cabin that could serve as a gun port, but he was convinced that a sudden attack from the road could catch them by surprise. With any luck, it would only be the women in the cabin, with the men occupying those stacked log positions and looking the other way.

Vincent planned to let two men attack from the rear and keep them occupied looking the wrong way. He would let the other two men storm the cabin and capture it. He would hang back while they did that, and once the cabin had been captured, he personally would pick off anybody trying to come back to the cabin from the log positions. Survivors, if there were any, would be put on a horse and told to get out of the area, and preferably out of the state. Satisfied with the plan he'd formed in his mind, Vincent put the field glasses away in his saddlebag and eased back into the trees.

Boone remained where he was at the foot of the plateau, concealed behind the barricade of tree limbs and brush he had constructed with McCabe. He remained completely motionless, watching through a chink in the barricade's wall as Vincent retreated, turned, and rode back toward the Diehl ranch. He remained unmoving for another ten minutes after Vincent had left, looking for any other signs of movement. Finally, he rose and began climbing the hill toward the cabin. Based on what he had just seen, he had a feeling there would be an attack by daybreak tomorrow.

———

Vincent began covering the plan with his men while Diehl listened in. They were sitting on the porch of Diehl's house. Diehl himself, Vincent noted, seemed almost uninterested in the details. Vincent looked at the men he had hired for the job, feeling some minor misgivings about this entire operation. The defensive position of the cabin was much stronger than he had expected, and the old man from the saloon and the one-legged ex-soldier both looked a little saltier than what he had been led to believe. His brief encounters with each of them at the saloon made him think they would both stand their ground and fight. McCabe might be out of the picture, but then again, maybe he wasn't. Still, they had the element of surprise on their side.

He looked around at the men he had hired, using the nicknames he had given them, since he could never be bothered to learn their actual names.

"Blondie, you and Butch," he said, pointing at the biggest of the four men, "will use the cover of the trees to work your way from the Diehl property onto their property. Don't expose yourself to fire until you're in close and then watch for fire from these positions at the top of the plateau."

He turned to a large piece of wrapping paper he had nailed to a board and propped up against the wall of the house. He sketched in the shape of the plateau and outlined the places where he had noticed the stacks of firewood.

"One or two of them might be pretty handy with a rifle," he cautioned.

Neither man looked particularly impressed with that last remark.

"Their funeral," Vincent muttered under his breath.

Turning to the other two men, Vincent first sketched in the trail leading from the road and the outline of the cabin.

"You two," he barked, "Fred, and uh, Skip. You're going to come in off the trail and rush the house. There might be a shot or two through a gun port in that cabin, so don't dawdle when you come around the bend. Stay low and stay under cover as long as you can. I'll lay down some fire to back you up. Get in the cabin and take out whoever is in there. Take 'em alive if you can. If anybody falls back from those log stacks to the cabin, I've got you covered. We're goin' in at daybreak. Meet right here one hour before daybreak tomorrow. Anybody got questions?"

Nobody said anything. Vincent scanned his four men. A couple of them were studying the sketch he had made on the paper. The other two silently returned his stare. Vincent shrugged and turned to look at Diehl, who was staring off in the distance and looked bored. Vincent waved at his hired help.

"You can go," he said.

When the others had left the porch, Diehl looked at Vincent.

"Your job isn't done when you've driven 'em off and cleared my grazing land," he reminded Vincent. "Your job is done when McCabe is dead. Assuming Karras can't get the job done."

Vincent nodded. "I can take care of both Karras and McCabe if Karras doesn't get the job done. Karras will cost you an extra two fifty."

Diehl wheeled around, but his protest died on his lips when he looked at Vincent, standing with his hands on his hips. "Okay," he muttered, "another two fifty for Karras." He stalked into the house.

Diehl sank into a chair in the library, wondering if he was in it too deep this time. He didn't want Vincent to have power over him when this was done. He was barely hanging on to this land—the truth was, he had paid the minimum amount to the bank on the loan he'd acquired to buy this land. He'd built the house, and he was running cows, which had cost him something. He saw no reason to make payments to the bank when he had the sheriff to stop foreclosure, and he had no plans to pay them anything more. A lot might depend on Daniels being re-elected as sheriff, but Daniels knew too much about him too and was getting more expensive all the time. He went looking for his whiskey again, then checked to make sure his cash was still in the side drawer of his desk. This morning he had sold a couple hundred head of cattle to a man organizing a drive to Kansas. He might sell a couple hundred more, he told himself. Cash money could come in handy.

———

Boone relayed his news at dinner with the Hawkins family that evening. He recounted watching the man in the trees, emphasizing how thoroughly he had looked the place over with his binoculars. Boone felt certain he had seen the man in the saloon in town, and he told the family that there had been four others with the man while he was in the saloon. He looked around the table when he had finished.

"If you folks still want to stay, there's gonna be a fight," he said. "I'll fight with you if you choose to stay."

Ike remained uncharacteristically silent, waiting for someone else to speak up. This, he knew, was too important for him to decide for all of them. Julia took in the surrounding faces in a glance. The boys were already fighting mad after Jake's horse had been stolen. The only question, she knew, was about her mother. Eventually, all eyes drifted to Jeanne, who was staring down at the table. Finally, she lifted her eyes to look at Ike.

"Where is that old Navy Colt of yours?" she asked.

Ike thumped the table as he stood and leaned over to give Jeanne a kiss.

"Everybody get some sleep if you can," he ordered. "Isaac, you and I are at the rifle pit on the far side of the cabin. Pete, you're at the other one. If you hear any shooting behind you, get over to join us. We'll have cover from the cabin over there. Boone, you're at the barricade down below, right?"

Boone nodded, and Ike continued, "Jeanne, you and Julia will be in the cabin. Julia, use your Winchester through the gun port. Jeanne, you'll have the Navy Colt. We'll be in position well before dawn. I'll be on watch until then. At dawn, we're ready." He stopped. "Questions?"

There weren't any. Ike began handing out the guns.

————

A gentle touch on the shoulder from Ike awakened Julia. She took a moment to get oriented, then swung to her feet and looked around for her mother. Isaac and Pete were walking out the door, carrying their rifles. Boone, she assumed, was already down below at the barricade. Jeanne was now on her feet, letting Ike check the Navy Colt to be sure it was loaded. Julia walked over to the cabin wall and picked up her new Winchester '73. There was no need to check to be sure it was loaded. She had checked it a dozen times last night.

"How much time do we have?" she asked, as her

father swung toward the door, crutches under his arms and his rifle slung over his shoulder.

"Maybe an hour," Ike told her, and then he left.

Julia swung the bolt on the door shut after Ike had left, then peaked through the gun porthole in the cabin wall. It was still too dark to see anything out there. She set the rifle down, leaning it against the wall. Every minute or two, she checked outside, trying to pick up any movement. She found it ironic that they had just arrived in Texas and were already in a range feud, which threatened to erupt into a range war at any moment. Jake had left Kentucky after a long-running feud up there, hoping to leave that all behind. He was likely to return home to find another feud in progress here. Maybe the McCabes had more than their share of bad luck. Then again, she was determined to help Jake change that luck.

Boone was hunched down behind the barricade at the foot of the plateau again. He had been there for a couple hours already, since he hadn't been able to sleep all that well during the night. He didn't know whether he should hope he'd been right about this attack coming today. On the one hand, if they were coming, they might as well get it over with now. If they weren't, he had upset and alarmed this family for nothing. His mind drifted back to a book his mother had read to him when he was a little boy. Something about a chicken who always thought the sky was falling. He tried to think of that chicken's name, but it just wouldn't come to him. Whatever. He just didn't want to be that chicken.

A noise from above and to the left told him that Ike was taking up his position behind the firewood up there. Boone wasn't even going to worry about anybody sneaking up on him from behind. His job was to concentrate on what lay out in front of him. He felt pretty sure they were going to come through the woods between here and Diehl's land. The moonlight hadn't been enough to help him until now, and the gray morning light was just beginning to give him some visibility out there. He concentrated on focusing on one object at a time, counting on being able to spot movement from the corners of his eyes.

As more light filtered through the trees, Boone noticed an occasional twitching of low-hanging tree limbs and underbrush. Swinging his gaze to the last place he had seen movement, he focused on an imaginary line of progress from that place in the underbrush to his current position. After a few minutes, he wasn't yet convinced if anybody was coming. If they were, he had to admit to himself that they knew enough to take it very slowly. He waited for a little more light and remained focused on his imaginary line through the trees. From time to time, he cast a glance to either side. If there was over one man out there, he couldn't afford to get over-whelmed by a rush from several positions.

After a few more minutes crawled by, Boone knew he couldn't afford to wait much longer. He concentrated on whatever he could find that looked out of place. Someone seemed to be coming, but not in a completely straight line. They had the sense to move a bit from side to side. Boone hunched over and sighted down the barrel, adjusting the rifle and focusing on details. There! A slight movement in the underbrush. Boone focused on a patch of color that seemed unnaturally dark. Mostly, he could see green leaves and underbrush, with an occasional dark tree trunk. This looked like a patch of black...Boone held his breath, exhaled slowly, and squeezed off a shot.

There was a muffled noise in front of him and a man rose slightly from the underbrush, taking aim to return fire. Boone fired again, striking the man squarely in the chest and driving him backward. Almost immediately, there was fire from across the pasture to his left, striking the logs on the barricade. Boone ducked instinctively, then looked through the chink in his barricade at the man he'd shot in front of him. That man was down and not moving. Another shot sounded from his left, then two rifles boomed from above and behind him.

Boone didn't dare raise his head above the cover provided by his position. He crawled to his left and risked a glance around the edge of the logs stacked in front of him. A rifle sounded again, to his left and in front. Now, he could see a man crouching in the thick brush, aiming his rifle upward at the firewood stack above. Boone took aim and fired. The man fell to his side, clutching his shoulder. Still holding his rifle, he came to his feet and lurched toward the cover of a thick oak tree. Two rifles sounded as one, from behind him and above, on the plateau. The man staggered back against the tree trunk, then slowly slid down the side of it. Boone held his position behind the barricade. Two men down. How many more of them were out in front of him?

Back in the cabin, Julia heard the gunfire behind her. Almost immediately after they fired the first shots, she could see two men burst out from behind the oak trees and run toward the cabin. She swung the rifle to the one closest to her and pulled off a quick shot—too quick, she could see that right away. He dropped his rifle and grabbed his arm, then picked it up and ran again. Meanwhile, the other man fired two shotgun blasts through the leather hinges on the door, first high and then low.

The door swung ajar. He dropped the shotgun and continued running, pistol in hand now. Julia centered on the chest of the first man she had fired on, and her second shot brought him down.

Now, the second man had burst through the door. Julie swung the rifle to cover him, but she didn't pull the rifle back far enough on the first try. The barrel was still stuck in the gun port. She pulled back violently and swung the rifle again, but she could see that she was too late. His pistol was coming up...a shot sounded loudly, and Julia jumped in surprise. She levered the Winchester and lined up her sights on him, but he was staggering backward. He fell out through the cabin door, and only his boots showed from where she was standing.

Uncomprehending, Julia swung the rifle to look behind her. Jeanne was standing, semi-crouched, holding the Navy Colt in both hands. A wisp of smoke curled up from the barrel. "This is my home," she said in a very soft voice.

# CHAPTER 15

## REGROUPING

J ulia saw that Jeanne had taken a seat after the shooting, but she had hung on to the Navy Colt and kept it trained on the door. Julia returned to the gun port in the wall and kept a watch on the clearing in front. After several minutes of silence, she could hear her brother Pete calling to them, and it sounded like he was coming up along the side of the cabin. He entered a moment later, his eyes wide with shock at the sight of the two corpses. A few minutes later Isaac entered the house also, followed by Ike in another ten minutes. The silence that had prevailed since Jeanne had shot the second intruder still seemed strange after the eruption of gunfire.

Julia looked around at her father. "Where is Boone?" she asked.

Ike jerked a thumb over his shoulder in the direction of the firewood stack at one end of the plateau. "Boone's come up the hill, but he's keeping watch over that pasture for a little while longer. Boone said there were five of 'em to start with, and we've only accounted for four so far."

Julia, confused for a moment, remembered then the sound of rifle fire out back before the two men had rushed into the cabin. "Accounted for?" She looked at Ike for an answer.

Ike grunted briefly and settled himself in a chair. "There's two more out there in the woods," he answered. "They're just as dead as these two. Boone nailed the first one, then flushed the other one out in the open." He stared at the second intruder, still laying over the doorstep. "Dang, it just don't pay to mess with the women in this family."

Ike waved a hand at Pete. "Take your rifle and spell your sister at that gun port. Keep an eye out front. There might be one more and there might not be."

Ike got up and went to the door, struggling to balance on his crutch while attempting to drag the second man outside. Julia went over and helped him pull the body over next to the other one, laying in the center of the yard. She watched as Boone finished a perimeter check, including an inspection of the tracks leading in from the road. They all came inside and sat in a circle, except for Pete, who maintained a watch.

Boone gave them his summary: "I think there was five of 'em that came at us. The two out yonder in the woods were just supposed to be a diversion, supposed to make us think they were comin' at us from that side. Those two are dead out there in the woods—I checked 'em out a while ago. Three of them came from in the front. Two charged the house and"—he glanced out at the yard"—they got dead, too. That just leaves the other one out front. Judging by the tracks out there, he skedaddled after things didn't go right." He paused to think for a minute. "That last one is probably the leader of the bunch, the one I saw in the saloon a couple times. The other four that came in town with him are all lyin' out there." He waved a hand vaguely toward the front yard and pasture in back. This was an uncharacteristically long speech for Boone, and he fell silent.

Ike looked around the room, then his gaze fell back on Boone.

"What do I do now?" he asked. "If I was back home in Kentucky, I guess I would report this to the sheriff. The sheriff here belongs to Diehl. No tellin' what he'll do if I report this."

Boone pondered the question, standing up to pace the room as he did so.

"Tell you what," he said, "give me a couple hours to get back in town and tell the story a bit around town. I'll tell 'em at the saloon and the general store, maybe a couple other places. The town don't like Diehl or Daniels —you'll have their sympathy." He started toward the door, then turned back. "The other thing is, you go to town and report it to Daniels, but stop off at the telegraph office first and report it to the Texas Rangers. It's really the sheriff's job to look into it, but the Rangers really don't like range wars. It's bad for folks moving in to settle, like you done here. Daniels and maybe Diehl, too, will get worried about the Rangers lookin' over their shoulders. That'll give 'em both something to think about." He left abruptly. Moments later, they could hear him riding out of the yard.

———

Al Vincent remained in front of the cabin for only a minute or two after he saw his two men go down in the yard. His plan had been to provide cover for those two after they gained access to the cabin, hopefully picking off the one-legged veteran and maybe even the old man from the saloon when they fell back to the cabin. Instead, both of his men had been gunned down trying to reach the front door. He mounted and rode back to the meeting point he had established with the first two men. Their job was to distract the settlers by firing from the woods surrounding the back pasture, then fall back to the edge of the Diehl land, where they were to meet Vincent.

Vincent waited at the meeting point for an hour, then another hour. He had heard the firing going on from the gun pits on the plateau, but that was part of the plan. His men would draw fire to distract the settlers, then fall back to this meeting point. When the second hour passed without the first two men falling back to meet him, Vincent realized that, unbelievably, all four men had been killed in the attack. He realized there was at least one defensive position on the property he had missed, and what was worse, they had expected the attack.

Vincent rode toward Fredericksburg. He wasn't yet prepared to report the morning's events to Diehl. He needed a plan first. He wasn't afraid of Diehl, but he prided himself on always getting the job done. He decided he would concentrate first on taking out McCabe, wherever he was, then he would take care of the old man at the saloon. He would get a few more men and go after the settlers again. He decided to give it a few hours, then go out and talk to Diehl. The man wouldn't be happy, but that was just too bad. The next time would go better.

———

Boone had done his job well in town. The story about the attack on the Hawkins family was the talk of the town, from the saloon to the general store. A crowd was currently gathered around Boone in the saloon as he recounted the story for the seventh time, by Boone's count. When he reached the part about the mother and daughter defending themselves against gunslingers and murderers in their own home, an angry buzz sounded from the crowd and glances were directed toward Sheriff Chase Daniels, sitting in the corner with his hat pulled down low over his forehead. He slammed down his whiskey angrily and left the saloon.

Stalking down the street, Daniels became more and more angry at the position Diehl had placed him in. He knew that the hired guns were being paid by Diehl, who was counting on Daniels, as sheriff, to cover up the problem. That the election was only one week away doubled the problem for him. He owed the sheriff's job to Diehl, whose money and backing had made it possible. On the other hand, if he didn't move against these men who had invaded the Hawkins' ranch, it wasn't likely he could be re-elected. How was he supposed to deal with this?

Daniels paused outside the jail, trying to decide what, if anything, he could do about it. If and when Hawkins reported the attack, he had to at least put on a show of investigating. He could find a way, somehow, not to connect it to Diehl, but the town wouldn't be happy about that. He wondered if he could blame it on Hawkins and McCabe. McCabe, he reminded himself, hadn't even been seen around here for several days. Looking up, he saw Ike Hawkins swinging out of the telegraph office on his crutch. He climbed into the seat of his buggy. Daniels decided on the spot to take the offensive and see how much of this he could blame on Hawkins.

As the buggy pulled away into the street, Daniels stepped out into its path and held up a hand. Hawkins pulled up on the reins and stopped the buggy. "Hawkins," Daniels shouted. "What's this I hear about a shooting on your ranch? Why haven't you reported it?"

Hawkins kept both hands in plain sight and stared down thoughtfully at the sheriff.

"Why, Sheriff," Ike said, as mildly as he could manage, "I was just on my way now to report it to you."

Daniels noticed, with some discomfort, that people were spilling out of the saloon to listen to the conversation.

Daniels was losing steam and had the uncomfortable feeling that the crowd could turn on him at any time, but he made one more try. "Why didn't you come to me right away?" he barked. "What was so important at the tele-graph office?"

Ike raised one hand in the air apologetically. "Sorry, Sheriff," he said. "I stopped first to telegraph a report to the Texas Rangers. I'm new around here," he added. "I didn't know who to report it to first," Ike concluded with an angelic smile.

Daniels took a step back. The mention of the Rangers had the exact effect that Boone had hoped for. Regrouping mentally, Daniels waved toward the jail. "Okay, Hawkins," he said, "you can come into my office here and give me your side of this story."

An angry buzz sounded from the crowd, and Daniels noticed they were forming a semi-circle around Hawkins's buggy.

"You can, er, tell me about the attack," he amended.

Ike grinned, pulled the wagon over and climbed down. Daniels held the door open for him, and glancing back, he saw that several people remained near the buggy.

———

Sitting behind his desk in the front room of the jail, Daniels went through the motions of interviewing Ike Hawkins. Butter wouldn't melt in this guy's mouth, Daniels thought sourly as he scribbled down a few notes on a pad of paper. He glanced out the window from time to time. There seemed to be several people who had no intention of leaving Hawkins's buggy until the man came back out. Daniels glanced up from time to time as Hawkins spoke. This was all just for show. He knew that the five men involved had to be Al Vincent and the four men he brought to town. He thought back to his confrontation with Vincent in the saloon several days ago. He hoped that Vincent was one of the dead ones. When enough time had gone by and he had scribbled enough notes, he ushered Ike Hawkins out the door, assuring him he, Sheriff Daniels, would look into this. Both men knew that wasn't true.

After Hawkins had left, Daniels stood indecisively for a few minutes, then began pacing the front office area. There wasn't a lot of room—he made about ten round trips from his desk to the coffeepot and back. Finally, he confronted Diehl about what had happened. He picked up his hat and jammed it on his head, slamming the door shut behind him as he left the town jail.

He put in a fifteen-minute hard ride to Diehl's ranch.

His horse was beginning to lather up in sweat as he dismounted in front of the house. He charged through the front door without knocking and followed the sound of voices into Diehl's library. To his dismay, he found Diehl, apparently already angry, talking with Al Vincent. Diehl rose from behind his desk with an angry stare. Vincent circled around to stand to his left. Daniels knew uncomfortably that he had overstepped. Some anger seeped out of him, but not all.

Diehl remained standing, his angry stare and silence demanding an answer for the intrusion. "There was an attack at the Hawkins' ranch," he spluttered. "Four men dead, the entire town is sympathetic with the Hawkins family." He paused, expecting some kind of answer. Diehl remained mute and unmoving. "Election next week and this happens," he continued after a moment. "And it had to be the guys you hired. The ones that came to town with..." His voice trailed off and he glanced over at Vincent, who took a step closer and hooked his thumbs into his gun belt.

Diehl slowly circled the desk until he was face-to-face with Daniels, who took an uncomfortable step back. Diehl stepped forward and closed the gap, keeping his face inches away from Daniels's face.

"Four guys I've never heard of attacked that ranch," he said, keeping his tone soft and menacing. "Four greedy guys who thought they could get some good ranch land for free. Thugs, ne'er-do-wells who got what they had coming. Al, here, overheard them talking about it in the saloon. He tried to talk them out of it, but they wouldn't listen to him. Is that about right, Al?"

Vincent smirked and leaned back against the wall, right hand still free and still hooked in the gun belt.

Chase Daniels shifted back and forth on his feet, looking from Diehl's angry face to Vincent's contemptuous face. The last of his anger drained away. Feeling threatened and not a little frightened, he turned for the door. The resentment would come later.

"Chase!" He cringed and stopped near the library door, half turning back to look at Diehl. "Nobody has seen McCabe in several days. I checked with the county clerk. If he hasn't been seen in another four days, they will remove his name from the ballot. You'll still be sheriff."

Daniels nodded briefly and left, jamming his hat on his head once he was out of the house. He was doubting that he wanted to be the sheriff anymore under these circumstances.

Diehl slowly circled back around and took a seat at his desk. He looked across the room at Vincent, who continued to lounge against the wall. His expression was only slightly less insolent than before. Diehl knew that he couldn't intimidate Vincent the way he had just intimidated Daniels, but he still needed some answers.

"You said you were going to make this right," he reminded Vincent. "How are you going to make this right? Hawkins is still on that land, and I know no more about McCabe than I did when you got here."

Vincent walked over to the end of the desk, picking up his hat and spinning it around with his left hand. "I always do what I'm paid for," he assured Diehl. "I'll wait for those four days you just mentioned and see if McCabe shows up. If he does, I'll take care of him before the election. Then I'll take care of Karras and I'll get a couple more guys to chase those settlers off. I know more about their defenses now, and they won't be expecting me next time." He put on his hat and left without waiting for a response from Diehl.

————

Clem Haskell had worked for the Texas General Land Office for many years now, and he liked the work. Nobody bothered him, the pay was decent, and he got to deliver good news to folks who needed good news. Several people had mentioned that he was getting older and maybe he should think about quitting, but he paid them no mind. He liked the feeling that he was helping people out. Take this man, Ike Hawkins, for instance. He had come to Texas to find some land for his family. Lost a leg in the war, apparently. Bought himself a little property near Fredericksburg with his hard-earned money and was looking for a grant of some land near it.

Clem bent over a map, using a magnifying glass to help with the small print. His map showed an area near Fredericksburg, and after studying the map for several minutes, he identified the small piece of land already owned by the Hawkins family. There was a marvelous piece of land, about the right size, just to the north of it, but that was apparently owned by a man named Diehl. There was no other land immediately next to the land already owned by Diehl, and that would do. Apparently, the other land bordering Hawkins's land was pretty heavily wooded, except Diehl's land to the north. He swung the magnifying glass to check the property to the west of Diehl's land. A small smile creased his face. This was one reason he really liked his job.

The property to the west of this man Diehl was available to be assigned by the state as a veteran's grant. The size was 1,300 acres. Twenty extra acres, but who was going to quibble about that? It looked like there might be a little water at the west end of the property. No direct access to the land they already owned, it didn't look like, but maybe they could work out an arrangement to cross the Diehl land, or maybe they could clear a path through the trees to connect the properties. He found a pen, dipped it in an inkpot, and made some notes about the location of the land. He walked over and dropped his notes into a basket on his boss's desk, who barely looked up.

With a small smile still on his face, Clem looked up at the clock at the far end of the room. The Hawkins were about to get a delightful piece of property. This was a good day so far. *Time for lunch*, he thought. He was going to try that new café down at the end of the street.

# CHAPTER 16

## JAKE'S TRAIL

J ulia opened a canvas bag on the bed and began tossing in a few items of clothing. She wasn't sure how long it was going to take to find Jake, so she decided to pack for a week. She packed steadily, intent on what she was doing. When Jeanne came over and placed the Navy Colt in the bag, she looked up in surprise.

"You might need it more than me," was all she said. Julia smiled briefly and finished packing. She knew the hard part would be telling Ike about it when he came home. At least her mother was in her corner.

The sound of the front door opening told her it was time for that discussion with Ike. She turned as her father came through the door and saw that he had spotted the bag on the bed. She did not try to hide the Navy Colt as Ike came over for a closer look. Ike turned away and swung across the room on his crutch, taking a seat in his favorite chair. He ran a hand through his short-cropped, grizzled hair and searched for the right words. He didn't seem to find any, opening his mouth to say something, then thinking better of it. Julia walked over and kneeled beside the chair, placing a hand on her father's arm.

"He's been gone too long, Dad. I have to see if I can find him."

Ike nodded miserably, staring at the floor.

"It could be really dangerous," he began. Then, he lapsed into silence again.

When he said nothing further, Julia realized that her father had resigned himself to the fact she would go. She sought to reassure him. "I'll be careful, Dad," she told him. "I need him here. We need him here. I can't just sit here if something has happened to him."

After a moment, her brother Pete entered the room, carrying a bucket of water. "Take Pete with you," Ike said finally. "Two are better than one. Boone and I will hold down the fort with Isaac and your mother." Pete set down his bucket of water and turned, looking at Julia for an explanation.

"I'm going to find Jake," she told him. "I guess you're coming with me."

Pete pulled a bag from under a bed. "Give me ten minutes," he said.

Pete beat his estimate: he was ready in five minutes. He carried Julia's Winchester '73 with him. Julia promised Ike they would be gone no longer than a week, and they soon cantered down the road and took the left fork, as Julia pointed out the places she had scouted a few days before. As they traveled down the trail, Pete fell silent, which was uncharacteristic for him. Julia glanced over.

"What's on your mind, Pete? Besides finding Jake, I mean."

Pete threw her a quick sideways look, then went back

to staring at the trail. "You shot one of those men in front of the cabin, right?"

She nodded.

Pete waited for a moment. "Do you still think about that?" he asked.

So that's what it's about, she thought. "I have trouble getting that picture out of my mind," she admitted. "But they were shooting at us and trying to force their way into the cabin. I don't know what else I could have done. Why?"

"Well..." Pete fiddled with the reins in his hand for a moment, "that second guy out there in the woods that Boone wounded. He came out of the brush. I saw him first and fired. Dad swung his gun around and shot at the same time, but his rifle wasn't aimed yet. I'm the one who killed him."

Julia pulled in on the reins and stopped her horse in the trail. Pete did likewise. She reached over to put a hand on his shoulder. This was a lot, she thought, for a sixteen-year-old boy to deal with. She was having enough trouble at age twenty-five.

"That was a hard thing," she said in a quiet voice.

He nodded, staring down the trail.

"They were coming after us, Pete," she reminded him. "They might have killed all of us, if we had let them."

He nodded his head unconvincingly.

"If you had it to do over, what would you have done differently?" she asked.

Pete turned that over in his mind. "I guess nothing," he said eventually. "I don't know what else I would have done."

She waited while he thought for a while longer.

Finally, he lifted the reins and clucked at his horse. "I want to find Jake," he said.

Julia moved up to ride alongside. She knew they would need to talk about it again. This was a start.

They spent another two hours drifting and scouring the ground for tracks. Julia spotted the place she had found on her first trip, where she thought Jake had probably made camp for the night when he passed this way. They both dismounted and searched the old campsite, but found nothing to help them. They re-mounted and pushed on until late in the afternoon. Luckily, they found that the lack of traffic on this trail made it possible to pick up the tracks from time to time.

They pushed on until they lost light with the sun dipping down below the trees in the west, and they searched for a likely place to make camp. Rounding a bend suddenly, they came upon a confusing grouping of tracks in the trail. Julia dismounted and inspected what she saw. Instead of the usual set of tracks for one horse, and another set for two, there was a large area in the trail with multiple hoof prints, first leading off the trails, then back on and circling around. There were also tracks of a man's shoes and a small circular area where the dust in the trail seemed darker.

Moving a little farther down the trail, they again saw tracks of a man in the trail, near a small pile of brush and dead tree limbs. There appeared to be an old campsite a little way off the trail in the woods. She turned to see Pete inspecting the pile of brush and tree limbs.

"What do you think, Pete?"

He stepped back and looked over at her. "It looks a little like that place that Jake and Boone built down near the well. The one Boone was shootin' from when those men attacked us."

Julia bit her lip and stared back down the road. She had been thinking the same thing.

Walking back out to the trail, she took some comfort because she could see the tracks of a few horses continuing on up the trail. Maybe three horses like before. She was again thankful that there was so little traffic on this trail. They had seen no one else all day. She walked back to look at the campsite they had found.

"We may as well make camp here," she told Pete.

————

"I've been here almost a week, and I still can't remember much," I complained to Jed over some breakfast at the café. "How long did it take you?"

Jed shrugged. "Mebbe a week or two," he said eventually. "It's been a while since then." He sipped some coffee, then looked across the table at me. "You can't remember anything else?"

I shrugged in frustration. "I keep seeing the burning cabin and the dead man in the yard in front of it. I had that dream again last night. In my dream, I yelled 'Russell.'" I stared out the window. "Russell," I repeated. I suddenly saw the dead man's face, but this time, the man was alive, sitting in front of a cabin and smiling. "He's my brother. Was my brother, I mean. Russell was my brother. Somebody killed him."

Jed watched me keenly, waiting for something else. I was a little stunned at what I had just remembered. Did I have any family left, I wondered? There was nobody else at that cabin in my dreams. Jed shoveled a forkful of eggs in his mouth and waited a little longer.

"Do you know where that was yet? Do any of the states we talked about the other day sound like someplace you been to? Arkansas, Kentucky, Tennessee, maybe Ohio?"

I rubbed my hand over my eyes and concentrated.

"Maybe Kentucky," I said uncertainly. "Not sure." I looked up. "How would I have gotten here clear from Kentucky without knowing anything about myself? Doesn't make sense."

Jed chewed thoughtfully, then put his fork down. "Mebbe you came here first, a while back," he suggested. "Mebbe you're rememberin' things that happened a while before. The war, the burned cabin, your brother, those are some powerful memories."

I thought that one over, then slowly nodded my head. That made sense. Jed fished around in his jacket pocket, then came out with a folded-up piece of paper.

"I was thinkin' about this before we came over here this mornin'," he said. "I remembered some older things first, myself." He finished unfolding the paper and pushed it across the table at me.

"What is it?" I asked, trying to make sense of what I was seeing.

"Map of Texas," he answered, picking up the fork and renewing his attack on the eggs. "Towns and rivers and such. See if any of it sounds like someplace you might have been."

I concentrated first on the rivers, sounding out the names and shaking my head at the sound of each one. I switched to the cities. A couple of them sounded a little familiar, but I figured I probably had already been familiar with the bigger towns, anyway. I traced a finger over the map, again sounding out the names in my head. My finger hovered over one name, then came down on the map with a thump.

"Fredericksburg," I said.

Jed's head came up. "Fredericksburg ain't far from here."

I tossed a couple coins on the table. Jed shoveled in the last mouthful and stood up.

"Where you goin'?" Jed asked.

"I've got one more appointment with the doc," I said as we left the café. "He'll see if I can get rid of this bandage around my head, and then I think I'll ride for Fredericksburg. Maybe there's something down there that can jog my memory a little." We parted ways, and I walked down to the doctor's office.

After a brief wait, the doctor brought me in for a look, unwinding the bandage around my head and examining the wound in the light. He made a couple of noises that sounded like "hmmm," and I waited impatiently for him to finish. He tossed the bandage in a trash can and sat back.

"Looks like it's healing up without a problem," he said. "How long ago did you come in here?"

"About a week ago," I said without hesitating. I had pretty much been counting those days.

"Okay," he said, standing up. "You can go without that bandage now. Are you remembering anything?"

I had started for the door, but I stopped to explain the dreams I'd had and how I could sometimes picture a face that I thought had been my brother. I finished by telling him the town of Fredericksburg seemed to be a name I recognized. "I think I'm going to ride down to

Fredericksburg now and see if I know anybody down there."

He nodded thoughtfully. "That might help," he agreed.

I turned again to go.

"But Bud," he said.

I waited at the door.

"Don't forget that you might be a man with enemies. They might be down there in Fredericksburg."

I left his office and started down the street toward the livery stable. Jed had said much the same thing to me a few days ago. It was something to keep in mind.

————

Karras was sitting in the saloon on the main street in Waco, drinking his breakfast. He stared glumly into his whiskey glass. He had arrived in town the day before last, pushing hard to get here before dark. He had thought it would be easy to find McCabe, or at least to find out if he had been in town and moved on. He had stopped at the first saloon he had found, which was down the street from this one, several blocks away. He had casually asked several customers in the saloon if they had seen somebody named McCabe, giving them a brief description. No one had heard of him.

Yesterday had been a repeat of the day before, although he had moved his search to this saloon, along with checking at the general store. Like before, nobody had heard of a Jake McCabe, and his description of a tall, dark man with dark hair had only brought a few shakes of the head. It had cut his questions in the café short when the sheriff appeared at the table next to him. He might have to move on down the road and keep looking somewhere else, he thought gloomily. But where? He had no idea where McCabe might have gone from here.

Looking across the saloon which had very few customers at this early hour, he saw one old man, who, judging by his appearance, might spend quite a bit of time in here. Karras sighed, finished his whiskey and moved across to stand over the old man, who looked up from an empty glass with watery eyes. Karras slid into the chair across from him.

"Buy you a drink, old-timer?" It was a measure of his desperation that he was willing to pay for the drink. The old man's eyes brightened, and he nodded his head in an uneven, slightly sideways motion.

"What kin I do fer ya?" The drink came and the old man transferred all his attention from Karras to the glass.

"You seen a man named McCabe in here, maybe the last week or so?" The old man downed the whiskey faster than Karras would have thought possible. He stared at the ceiling and scratched his chin absently.

"Nope. Can't remember nobody named McCabe."

Karras mumbled under his breath in frustration. "Tall man, dark hair, maybe thirty."

The old man started to shake his head no, then stopped, focusing on the wall and concentrating. "Well..." he said, looking hopefully at the empty glass. Karras stifled a curse and waved for another. The old man downed the new arrival as fast as he had the first one. "Don't know about no dark hair...kinda hard to tell what with the bandage around his head. Tall and dark. Wasn't named Jake McCabe, though. Bud somebody, I think." His head slumped down to rest on the table.

Karras sat straight upright, slapped some coins on the

table and jumped from his chair. Of course! Head wrapped in a bandage. Why hadn't he been asking about that all along? He trotted out to the street, looking up and down in both directions. The man could call himself anything he wanted, but the bandage around the head... that was going to be a dead giveaway.

———

Julia and Pete rode into town after two-and-a-half days of hard riding. At a certain point, after seeing the sign for Waco, they had stopped trying to follow tracks and had simply pushed to get to town. Julia had to admit to herself that she didn't know what to do if they couldn't find Jake here. First things first. She needed a bath and food, with food taking priority right now. She dismounted in front of a café, and she went in with Pete to order a meal.

As they finished eating, Pete asked the question she was struggling to figure out. "How do we find him?" he asked.

Julia stared out the window into the street. "Well," she began, then stopped and stared.

A man had walked past in the street who looked familiar. One of Diehl's gunmen, maybe. She frowned and tried to think of his name. Nothing came to her mind. She looked out again, but he had moved on. She shook her head. Maybe it was nothing. She looked up to find Pete staring at her quizzically.

"We just walk around for a bit, I guess, and ask a few people if they have seen him." Then another thought came to her. "Look for Sherman, too. Would you recognize his horse?"

Pete nodded his head slowly. "I can ride past some shops and check the hitching rails. I can look for Sherman and for Jake's brand."

Julia left some money, and they headed for the door. Another thought struck her as they reached the street.

"The livery stable. I'll check the livery stable. I saw it just a couple blocks down the street."

She left Pete and hurried down to the stable. She found an old man sweeping up when she entered. He looked at her, then looked around for her horse.

"No," she explained. "I don't need to leave my horse here. Not yet, anyway. I'm looking for a friend of mine. Name of Jake McCabe. He would have come in the last week or so. Do you know him?"

The old man shook his head emphatically. "Don't know nobody around here by that name." He turned around and resumed sweeping.

Frustrated, Julia made one more try, although she was talking to his back now. "Tall, dark hair, handsome man..." Her words trailed off, and she turned to go.

"Wait!" The old man had turned back around, muttering, "Dark-haired, pretty girl." Jed made a guess, taking a step closer to her. "You from Fredericksburg, by any chance?"

Julia's face registered her surprise. "Yes, I am. Why?"

Jed began to chuckle. "Bud, er...Jake has been working for me for about a week. He took a glancing shot to his noggin and lost his memory. He has been rememberin' a couple things these last couple days. One of 'em was a dark-haired, pretty girl. You fit the bill, ma'am. An' this morning he thought he might be from Fredericksburg." He chuckled some more, immensely pleased with himself. "If that don't beat all," he mumbled.

Julia resisted the urge to grab his collar and shake him for information. "Where IS he?" she demanded.

Jed stopped chuckling long enough to point down the street in the direction of the café.

"Went to the doc's office to get hisself checked out," he said. "Down that way about six or eight blocks. Sign says Dr. Abrams. Can't miss it." He went back to sweeping and chuckling.

Julia hurried back out to the street and down toward the doctor's office. She couldn't believe her good luck in finding him this fast. She wondered if Jake would recognize her when she found him. Apparently, he had been seeing her face in his mind, but probably couldn't remember her name. Or his, she reminded herself. She hurried a little faster.

Looking down the street, she saw him. She was sure it was Jake. She began waving to him, but he hadn't seen her yet. Suddenly, a man stepped off the sidewalk behind Jake. She had a better look at the man now. She was sure it was Diehl's gunman. She heard him call Jake's name. Jake's face registered both surprise and confusion, then he turned to look at the man. To her horror, she saw the gunman's hand drop and draw.

# CHAPTER 17

## BREAKTHROUGH

The warning from the doctor was still weighing on my mind as I started down the street. In my case, not only did I not know who my enemies might be, I didn't have any memory of why they were enemies, and no idea on how and when they might strike again. It didn't change my mind about a visit to Fredericksburg, but I would have to be on my guard all the time.

As I drew into the center of town, I saw a woman approaching me who looked familiar. I looked at the features and the dark hair, and thought she might be the woman I had pictured in my head a few times. As I watched, she seemed to wave at me. I quickened my pace, feeling very hopeful this was a genuine breakthrough in remembering my past. Plus, that was a pretty lady waving at me.

Suddenly, a voice behind me shouted, "McCabe!" Several thoughts rushed into my head at once. That name sounded so familiar—maybe that was my name! Who was shouting at me? What did they want? For the moment, I forgot even that beautiful woman headed in my direction. I turned, trying to sort out all the thoughts in my brain. When I turned, I saw a man with a gun in his hand, clearing the holster and raising it toward me. The practicing I'd been doing with Jed after work is what saved my life.

I dropped into a crouch and reached instinctively to draw my gun. I took an extra second to clear the leather and raise the gun, even as the angry whine of a bullet sounded in my ear. I leveled the gun, aiming for the center of his chest as I pulled the trigger. I saw the shot strike him and knock him backward, causing his second shot to fire harmlessly in the air. He brought the gun down as he fell backward, and I fired again, sending the second bullet under his chin as he dropped away from me. I knew he couldn't survive that second shot, but it took a moment to realize it was over. I was still crouched in the street, and he was stretched out on his back in the dust. Gradually I heard sounds and realized people on either side of the street were moving again. A few walked over toward the dead man, but nobody was approaching me.

I dropped my gun back into the holster, realizing now that the name he had called was my actual name. I was McCabe—Jake McCabe. I still didn't know who had shot at me. Everything had happened so fast. I heard my name again and turned to see the dark-haired woman I had seen before. Now, she was running toward me. I knew her!

"Jake!" She closed the last few steps and wrapped me up in a hug. She said my name again, and several images flashed through my mind. I was sitting with her on a bench outside a cabin. I saw her in the main street of a town, hugging me, just like she was doing now...

"Julia!" She pulled back and gave me a kiss.

"Yes! The man at the stable said you had lost your memory, and I was afraid you wouldn't know me." A huge smile spread across my face for the first time in many days.

"Just now," I told her. "Just now, I remembered."

She hugged me again, and I felt her stiffen. I knew she must be looking over my shoulder at the dead man in the street. The reality of what had just happened began to settle in on both of us. I turned, keeping one arm around her, and looked at the man in the street again.

"I don't know who that was," I told her. "He called my name, and I turned. He was shooting at me and I shot back." I lapsed into silence.

"He was Diehl's gunman," she said. "His name was Karras. Do either of those names sound familiar to you?"

I nodded. More was coming back to me now.

"He was shooting at me back on that property, where I built a cabin." I blinked a couple times. "Boone and I built a cabin...I was near the pasture down below there. Two guys were shooting at me. My shot grazed that one's shoulder, and I shot the other one through the leg."

I stood there with Julia, sorting through the memories and images in my mind. I could remember riding on the trail, coming here, turning a corner and blacking out. I remembered my stolen horse...Sherman. Now, I noticed some people gathering around us. A man with a badge stepped in front of me. I knew it was the sheriff. Jed had introduced us at the saloon one night.

"Sheriff Dullum," he reminded me. "Bud, right? Did you shoot that man?"

"I shot him," I acknowledged. "He called my name

and was firing at me when I turned. My name is McCabe," I added. "Jake McCabe."

He studied my face for a moment, then looked at the people who were ringed around us.

"Did anybody see this? Can anybody else tell me what happened?"

A tall man in a blacksmith's apron nodded his head. "Just like he said, sheriff. That man called him out and started shooting."

The sheriff turned and looked at Julia. "Ma'am, are you his wife?"

Julia blushed slightly.

"No," she said, "I'm a friend. I came up here looking for him when he didn't come home after a few days."

The sheriff looked at me again. "I need you to wait for me in my office for a few minutes," he said. "It shouldn't take long. I need to take care of that body over there and I'll just ask a few more questions." He turned to Julia.

"Ma'am, you can wait with him if you'd like."

He moved down toward the dead man, where a couple of men were already starting to load him onto a wagon. Dr. Abrams moved away from the corpse and came toward me.

"Looks like one of those enemies found you. Were you shot?"

I told him I was fine and moved to the steps in front of the jail. Julia climbed the steps with me, then stopped.

"Pete!" she blurted. "Pete came with me. I'll find him and bring him over." She moved away just as Jed came out of the crowd and followed me into the jail. I looked at him questioningly.

"I heard the shootin'," he said. "Folks out there told me you was the one done most of the shootin'. I can just tell the sheriff what I know about you. Won't hurt none, will it?"

I agreed it wouldn't hurt and actually felt a bit comforted by his presence.

The sheriff entered a few minutes later and looked at Jed. "What are you doing here?"

"This man has been workin' for me for the last week," he said. "Got bushwhacked on the trail on his way here. Couldn't remember nothin' about who he is nor what happened. He's been causin' no trouble. Just workin' for me and trying to remember who he is."

The door opened and Julia walked in, followed by Pete.

Jed brightened up. "Hey, pretty girl!" He looked at me. "Is she the one you remembered?"

I nodded.

"I knowed it!" he crowed.

The sheriff sighed and sat back in his chair. "Are you done, Jed? I'd like to ask a few questions. I'm the sheriff, remember?"

"Sorry," Jed mumbled.

The sheriff looked over at Pete, then at Julia. "Who is he?"

"He's my brother," Julia explained. "We'll just sit over here out of the way."

They took a seat, and the sheriff turned his attention to me. "Well," he said, "there were several people out there who told me it went down just the way you said. It sounds like he drew on you and you defended yourself. I don't have any plan to arrest you."

I sighed with relief.

"Do you know who that was?"

I glanced over at Julia. "I didn't really get much of a

look at him before the shooting, but Julia says he was a gun hand working for a rancher named Diehl, down where we live in Fredericksburg."

The sheriff wrote both names on a sheet of paper. "Is he the one who ambushed you on your way here?"

I frowned in concentration, then shook my head briefly. "I couldn't see the man," I admitted. "Whoever it was, he shot from ambush and I never saw him."

He nodded. "That's the way ambushes usually are. What do you plan to do now?"

"I'm going home," I told him. "Home to Fredericksburg."

He stood and walked us to the door. "I have no problem with that," he said. "You are welcome to come back here if you want to."

Jed and I waited while Julia and Pete found their horses, then we all walked down to the livery stable. I collected Sherman and the horse I had borrowed from Julia, then loaded on the few things I had with me.

"We need to check in with the county clerk in Fredericksburg first thing," Julia told me. I looked at her blankly. "The election," she said. "It is coming in less than a week. The election for sheriff."

I searched my brain and came up empty.

"That one, I don't remember. Why would I care about an election for sheriff?"

"Because you're running for sheriff," she explained. And why wouldn't you?" she asked. "You're a good man and obviously you can take care of things when you have to. The town needs you."

I started to protest, then shrugged in resignation and mounted up.

Jed chuckled. "Sounds like you're gonna be busy. You

come back and see me if'n you're in Waco again." He shook my hand, and we headed out on the trail home to Fredericksburg.

———

Sheriff Chase Daniels sat in his office chair, looking at the two Texas Rangers sitting across from him. He shifted uncomfortably, trying to remember the names they had given him when they walked in. He came up empty, but decided it didn't matter. He didn't like the way they were talking to him, and he figured he would try asking the questions for a while.

"Why are the Texas Rangers investigating a shooting in my county? I'm the sheriff here and I'm the one who will look into it." The one on the left, the one with the bright red hair and the penetrating stare, leaned forward and placed his elbows on the desk.

"Shootings," he said.

Daniels stared at him. "What?"

"Shootings. You said *shooting*. They killed here four men, and it sounds like a lot of shots were fired. The man over at the saloon said the wife and daughter killed two of 'em when they rushed the cabin. Pretty nasty stuff, it sounds like."

Daniels shifted uncomfortably again. "Yeah, okay, shootings. I'm looking into it, though. My office will take care of it." The one on the right leaned forward.

"What do you have?"

A few small beads of sweat appeared on Daniels's forehead.

"What?"

"What have you found out? It's been a week. What

have you found out so far? The governor doesn't much like range wars. Bad for people moving into Texas. What," he repeated, "have you found out so far?"

Daniels shuffled through some papers, pretending to read a few notes.

"Those guys that got shot were all from out of town," he announced.

The red-haired ranger looked over at the other one. "From out of town, he says. The old man at the saloon told us that didn't he, Phil?"

Phil nodded. "That's what he told us, Red. How long we been in town now? Half an hour?"

Red nodded his head solemnly. "Yeah, about a half hour, I'd say." Red returned his gaze to the sheriff. "I guess," he said, "we won't get anywhere here. We'll do a little looking around. If you have any complaints, you can write to the governor." They stood to leave.

Sheriff Daniels, now getting out his handkerchief to pat the sweat on his forehead, came to a decision. Diehl paid well, but he was a jerk, and Daniels would not go down with him.

"Wait," he said.

The Rangers turned back.

"Those settlers out there, they have a neighbor named Diehl. Diehl likes to graze his cows on their property." The two Rangers looked at each other.

"Now we're getting somewhere," said Red. They took a seat again. "What else?"

Daniels, not lifting his eyes from the desk, hesitated briefly. "There's a gun hand from out of town—Paris, Texas, I think—name of Vincent. Al Vincent."

The two Rangers exchanged glances.

"He was in the saloon with the four that got killed,

just a day or two before the shootings." He glanced up. "Maybe Diehl hired them. I'm not sure."

Red gave him the same penetrating stare as before. "It doesn't sound like you've been real busy with this case, Sheriff. Things really hopping here in Fredericksburg, are they? Keeping you busy with other things?"

Daniels cleared his throat nervously but said nothing. The two men stood again.

"Your choice, Daniels," said the red-haired one. "You want to come with us when we go out to talk to Diehl?"

Daniels kept his gaze on the desk. "No," he mumbled.

——————

Diehl was sitting on his front porch when two men with badges rode up. He forced a smile on his face and stood to greet them, knowing that his worst fears were coming to pass. Even if they couldn't tie him to the attack on the Hawkins property, the sweet deal he had going here with Daniels as sheriff was probably over. He owed the bank another $2,000 on this property, with at least $700 due immediately. That was manageable, of course, but not if he got arrested. He kept a forced smile on his face and waved them inside.

They introduced themselves, but the names were lost on him. His mind was racing. Sometimes, a man just needed to know when it was best to fold his hand and cash in. He ushered them into the library. They declined the whiskey he offered, but he poured himself a double and settled down behind his desk.

"What can I do for you, gentlemen?" he asked, the smile feeling frozen on his face at this point.

The red-haired man took his time, glancing around

the room and settling himself down into his chair. "Do you know a man named Al Vincent?" he asked suddenly.

A dozen thoughts raced through his mind, but the one that stayed with him with was this: Chase Daniels had sold him out to save his own hide. "Al Vincent." He stared at the ceiling vacantly and knitted his brows in thought. "Noooo..." he said slowly. "I don't believe I have met anyone with that name."

The two lawmen exchanged a look, clearly unconvinced.

"Did you know," the blonde-haired one said, "that there was an attack on the Hawkins' family?"

"Hawkins," Diehl said, trying to maintain the same vacant stare. A quick glance told him he was overdoing this.

"Oh, yes, the family who has settled in on the old Richardson place. Yes, I did hear about that. Terrible thing. I've been meaning to ride over and see if I can help. Maybe today."

There was a skeptical silence that followed. His gut told him they were trying to decide whether to take him out of here in handcuffs right now. They finally broke the silence with a few questions about how long he had been on this property, how many head of cattle he owned, and a few other general questions. Maybe, he thought, they were trying to decide if it was safe to leave him here until they could investigate a little more. If only they knew, he thought. One more chance was all he needed.

After a few more hard questions about any connections he might have to Paris, Texas, the red-haired one fixed him with that penetrating stare one more time.

"If I checked into your past, maybe to see if a man matching your description is wanted for a crime in Texas, do you think I would find anything? I'm assuming," he said bluntly, "that Virgil Diehl ain't the name your mama gave you when you were born."

Diehl choked slightly on his last gulp of whiskey. That was uncomfortably accurate. The shooting in Big Spring had been five years ago, and he had shaved his beard and mustache since then. Still, there might be a poster or a drawing floating around somewhere. Uncomfortable smile back in place, he assured them he had always been a law-abiding citizen.

"Uh-huh," said Red as they rose.

Diehl saw them out. This one more chance was all he needed. When they were out of sight, he called for Bates. The man has been worth nothing ever since the day McCabe had shot him in the leg. It was time to get some work out of him. His cattle buyer had told him he would buy four hundred more cattle at the $7 price he'd paid before, if Diehl wanted to sell. Together with the money from the last sale and what he had put in that drawer, it gave him about $8,000 to start over. California was starting to sound good.

When Bates came in, he gave the order to round up four hundred head to take to his buyer. He added casually that he would ride along. When Bates left, he began packing just a few things. Better to be able to ride hard, travel light, and buy what he needed later. There would be about four hundred head of cattle left on the property, but he couldn't help that. He valued his freedom too much.

———

Al Vincent lowered his binoculars and sat his saddle in the trees, watching Diehl and a few hands as they drove several hundred head of cattle off to the west. By his estimate, at least four hundred cattle had been driven away and probably sold. That left a few hundred more on the property. Things were shaping up better than he had imagined.

Earlier, back in Fredericksburg, he had just stepped out to the street in time to see two Texas Rangers come out of the sheriff's office. They had saddled up and moved out of town. On an impulse, he had followed, keeping well back. When it became obvious they were coming out to talk to Diehl, he had detoured into the woods and started watching the house. The Rangers had left after a half hour, and activity had started immediately afterward. They had rounded up some cattle, but not all. Now, as Diehl rode out with maybe half the cattle he still owned, Vincent wondered if the Rangers had scared him enough to cause him to cut his losses and run.

He stayed where he was for quite some time. This was as good a place as any for a man to think. He had only half his money from Diehl, but the cattle still out there would pay more than twice as much as a payoff on the job. Plus, he had the half Diehl had paid for the four helpers. Vincent had told them they wouldn't be paid until the job was done. With those four dead, he had pocketed that money. Maybe, he thought, he could hire a few cowboys and drive these cows as far as Ft. Worth. He might get $10 a head up there. He might even think about joining with another herd and taking them to Kansas. That would be a huge payoff.

Of course, he couldn't attract too much attention. He would have to get rid of McCabe. He felt sure Karras hadn't gotten the job done. He would have to get rid of that one-legged veteran, too, and maybe the old man from the saloon. Then, he could drive the family off and take the cattle with no one knowing about it for quite a while. He could walk away from this with at least $6,000. More than twice that if he got the cows to Kansas. A broad smile creased his face. He put the spurs to his horse and started back to town. He decided that he would give it three days before he made any moves.

# CHAPTER 18

## VINCENT'S PLAN

Two hard days of riding brought us close to Fredericksburg. I made sure we used a more well-traveled trail this time. We made camp on that second night only because it was too dark to continue. Sitting around the small campfire after dinner, Julia was again insistent that we ride directly into town and check in with the county clerk. I argued for a trip home first to clean up, but she told me that if we didn't get to town on time, Chase Daniels would automatically be the sheriff again. There wouldn't be anybody running against him on the ballet. This was a whole unknown world for me, running for sheriff. Back home, folks mostly just tried to keep the lawman away from the still.

Julia told me for the first time about the shootout at the ranch, the four dead gunmen, and the man named Al Vincent, who they thought was involved. She told me he hadn't been accounted for after the shooting was over. Daniels, she said, was the only one who was responsible for finding out who had done it, and he wasn't likely to do anything. I realized for the first time how important it was to get to town. The family would be lucky if Daniels didn't blame them for the shootings.

We moved at first light, and it was getting close to midday when we reached the streets of Fredericksburg. There was surprisingly little activity in town, but the county clerk was at his desk when we walked into his office. His face broke into a smile when he saw me.

"Dang, what a pretty sight," he said when we showed up.

I looked over at Julia.

"No." He grinned. "Ordinarily, I'd be talking about her, but in this case, I would have needed to remove you as a sheriff candidate if you hadn't rolled in before five o'clock. Nobody had seen you around here in more than a week. More of us are rooting for a change in the sheriff's office."

I looked around blankly and spread my hands in front of me, not sure what to say. "Well," I told him eventually, "I'm back and I plan to stay. Maybe sometime I can explain what happened to me."

"Not a problem for me," he said. "The election is in three days. You just need to be here then." As we turned to go, he called out to me, "Oh, and Jake, I'd suggest you let yourself be seen around town so people know you're back. Maybe show up at the general store and the saloon, let folks from out of town see you too. The sheriff is elected by the whole county."

I waved at him, and we walked out. I had to admit it —the saloon sounded like a good idea.

Boone let out a bellow when we walked through the doors. Julia told Pete to go on home and let the family know that I was back. Boone charged across the floor, stopping to pull out a chair for Julia.

"Where you been?" he started.

I took off my hat and set it on the table. Boone looked at the wound on the side of my head, still healing.

He let out a whistle. "Where'd that come from?"

I filled him in briefly on the ambush, and how my memory had deserted me for a while. He sat back and whistled again while I took a pull on my beer.

"Who done it?" was his next question.

I shrugged. "Julia says it was Diehl's gunman, Karras. I didn't really get a good look at him."

He thought that one over.

"Where's Karras now? He ain't been around here for a while."

I finished my beer.

"He's in a pine box up in Waco. We had a little—uh—disagreement."

Boone leaned against the back of his chair.

"Well," he said eventually, "if that don't beat all. Karras is gone and Diehl too, since a few days ago."

It was our turn to be surprised. Julia's mouth formed a small *O* at the news.

Boone, enjoying the attention, started to fill us in. "Word is," he began, "that two Texas Rangers showed up in Chase Daniel's office a few days ago. I didn't think anybody would really come when I suggested to Ike that he telegraph the Rangers. I just figured maybe Daniels and Diehl would have to keep their heads down an' stay neutral. Word is, them Rangers rode out to see Diehl after they saw Daniels. And get this. He gathered up some cattle and drove 'em off. Maybe gonna sell 'em. He hasn't been seen since, and that was, uh, mebbe three days ago. An' them Rangers took off after him, we think. They disappeared too. Daniels ain't hardly come out of his office since."

Boone finished his story, looked around, and thumped the table for emphasis. He was clearly enjoying the surprise and attention he was getting by telling us the news. Julia and I stared at each other, with brief smiles forming on both our faces. Both Karras and Diehl, apparently, were out of the picture. Daniels was staying out of sight. Maybe, I thought, McCabe's luck was changing for the better. Then, another thought struck me.

"What about Al Vincent?" I asked. "What became of him?"

Boone's smile faded, and he shifted in his seat. "Yeah, that's the other thing," he said. "Nobody'd seen hide nor hair of him for several days, but he showed up here in the saloon, just about an hour ago. Had a beer at the bar and left without sayin' nothing to nobody. Seems like maybe he just wanted to be seen. No idea where he went. Just rode out of town, somebody told me." He stared at the floor and frowned, then looked back up at me. "He's poison mean, Jake. You might need to watch out for him. Won't dry-gulch you like Karras, but he's salty. Mighty salty."

Julia covered my hand with hers. She looked as disturbed as I felt.

"What's this guy look like?" I asked. Boone shrugged. "Tall, dark hair, always wears a big sombrero-lookin' hat. Scar on the right cheek. Wears a Colt .45 pistol. I think you'll know him if'n you see 'em. He'll want you to know it's him."

Spirits somewhat dampened, Julia and I rode out to the ranch. There was almost no conversation between us for the first half of the ride. The news that Vincent, who was the most dangerous one in the whole bunch, was still around, bothered us both. If Diehl had paid him to get rid of us and Diehl was gone, why would Vincent still be around? Neither of us had an answer for that one, but our spirits rose as we got closer to the property. Maybe, we thought, Vincent would just ride out.

Jeanne saw us first when we pulled into the yard and yelled into the house at Ike, who swung out on his crutch, beaming with delight. The family surrounded me as I swung down, giving me hugs and telling me how delighted they were to see me. I caught Julia's eye and grinned. She laughed and gave me another hug. It occurred to me that I hadn't been welcomed home like this in a good many years.

Ike took me to the back of the plateau and showed me the cattle that were grazing near the pond. They were clearly Diehl's cattle, but they had seen neither Diehl nor any of his men. The cows had pretty clearly come for the water. Ike was just letting them graze, waiting to hear something more about Diehl. So far, he had been content to leave them alone. It raised the question in our minds of who they belonged to if Diehl didn't return. Neither of us had an answer for that one.

———

Vincent had decided that last night would be the final night he would spend camping in the trees bordering Diehl's pasture. Diehl had left a few days ago, and Vincent felt convinced he would have returned by now if he planned to come back. He had, Vincent felt sure, sold those cows he had driven out of here and moved on. Even the hands working on his ranch were all gone now.

The one thing that was still a cause of concern had to do with the presence of the two Rangers. He would keep an eye out for them when he returned to Fredericksburg today. He was done hiding out, though.

Meanwhile, he wanted to get a better idea of how many cows Diehl had left behind. They were a payday on the hoof out there, just waiting for him to cash in. He took his binoculars from his saddlebag and sauntered to the south, where they all seemed to have gathered around the pond on the settler's land. He moved very cautiously, scanning the plateau above him and in front. It seemed like the one-legged vet and the old coot from the saloon could shoot pretty well.

When he got to a good vantage point, he slung the binoculars around his neck and counted. Ten minutes later, he took a recount and came within five of the same number. Somewhere around 410 head of cattle remained. Satisfied, he retreated to the campsite of the previous two nights and struck camp. He planned to stay in a hotel from now on.

Once on the trail to Fredericksburg, he gave some thought to how he wanted to proceed with the next part of his plan. He needed to take out McCabe first, assuming Karras hadn't already killed him. The election was in a few more days, and if McCabe had returned, there didn't seem to be much doubt that he would be the new sheriff. He didn't expect Daniels to support him after he shot McCabe. He didn't expect Daniels to do anything, and that was all he needed. Tomorrow, he decided, would be the day. There would be plenty of time after that to deal with Ike Hawkins and Boone.

He turned his thoughts to how he wanted to kill McCabe. He had never shot a man from ambush, and he never would. He had killed more than a dozen men, but they had all had a chance. He might look for little things to give him the advantage in a gunfight, but he never shot from ambush. That was for cowards. No, he would need to call out McCabe face-to-face in Fredericksburg. Nobody could say it hadn't been a fair fight. He touched his spurs to his horse and picked up the pace into town.

———

Julia reminded me, shortly after breakfast, that I had been advised to show up in town every day to let people know that I was back. The county clerk, she reminded me, had told me it was important. I grumbled a bit, but had to admit she was right. I prepared to head into town, and she announced that she would go with me to buy some supplies. That cheered me up some. We hitched up the wagon and started into town. Julia scooted over next to me on the seat.

"You'll be doing this a lot after you're elected sheriff," she told me. "I'll come along with you sometimes." That was a pleasant prospect. We rode on into town, the morning air still just a bit cool.

I spent a couple hours just walking around the streets of Fredericksburg, meeting a few people I hadn't met before, but mainly just stopping to talk to people I had come to know during my time around these parts. Shortly before noon, Julia went across the street to buy some things at the general store, and I stopped into the saloon to see Boone. He told me that Daniels mainly stayed in his office at the jail these days, and he also told me that Diehl had apparently gotten out of the state. The word was that he had caught a train to California before the Rangers had caught up with him.

Feeling mildly disappointed with the news about Diehl, I left the saloon and crossed the street, looking for Julia. A voice to my left stopped me.

"McCabe! I've come for you!"

I looked over to see a tall man, dressed completely in black, standing in the middle of the street. I took a couple more steps to get the direct sun out of my eyes. I knew vaguely that Julia had stepped out of the general store, and that people had stopped moving. Some were backing up against the storefronts, afraid of stray bullets.

The morning sun behind him lightened the left side of his face, causing a large scar on his cheek to stand out prominently. I didn't need to ask. This, I knew, must be Al Vincent. I returned his stare.

"What's your problem with me?" I asked. "I've never met you."

He chuckled mirthlessly. "I don't need a reason. You're wearing a gun, and I'm callin' you out."

We both stood for a long moment, neither of us moving.

Suddenly, a door slammed down the street somewhere, and he flinched, momentarily distracted. I dropped into a crouch, and my hand swept down for my gun. I was still clearing leather when his gun boomed, and I felt a blow strike my left shoulder. I staggered backward, half turned by the shot, but managed to steady down, line up on his chest, and pull the trigger. He fell back a couple steps but fired again, and I felt a stab of pain in my leg.

I dropped to my knees and fired. The bullet turned him and he fired high, then brought his gun down again.

I steadied myself and fired twice, each shot striking him in the middle of the chest. He dropped the gun but somehow stayed on his feet, a blank look of confusion on his face. Finally, after an impossibly long time, he staggered and fell face down in the street. I dropped my gun, feeling a wave of nausea pass over me.

I knew Julie was there, kneeling in front of me. I fell forward into her arms, too weak to stay up on my knees anymore. I could sense people gathering around us. Julia was whispering to me now.

"Stay with me, Jake. Stay with me."

I nodded my head, but I didn't seem to be able to say anything. I could hear Boone's voice.

"Give 'em room. Back off!"

Somewhere along the way, I stopped hearing the voices around me, and the morning light faded.

# CHAPTER 19

## BOONE'S BRAINSTORM

THREE WEEKS LATER...

I watched Julia crossing the yard with a pitcher of lemonade, and I sank a little deeper in the chair Boone had rigged up for me. I had to admit I was getting pretty spoiled. The first week after the shootout, I'd had to stay in a bed at the doctor's office, and I was glad that was over with. I had wanted to get around on a crutch, the way Ike did, but the shoulder wound and leg wound were both on my left side, so I'd had to wait for my leg to get well enough to get around on it a bit.

I'd had a little luck on my side during that gunfight, I had to admit. Vincent had been quick—I had known right away that he was faster than me. And I had found out the hard way that he didn't go down easy. The one thing I had done right was to take enough time to make the first shot count. That had been the difference.

Julia set the pitcher down, gave me a kiss, and settled down on the ground next to me. I took a sip of the lemonade and sighed. It was almost going to be a shame when I got well enough to start doing my new job. Chase Daniels had left town after word got out that I was going to heal up from my wounds. They told me I had gotten over seventy percent of the votes for sheriff. I knew that a lot of them were just voting against Daniels, but I intended to do a good job for them. I looked around me.

"Where are Ike and the boys?" I asked.

Julia pointed to the north and west. "Out looking over our new land," she answered.

Word had come through about a week ago that Ike and his family had been given a land grant of 1,300 acres. The property was adjoining the Diehl land on the west. I had seen a map of it, but hadn't been able to ride out and see it yet. I was determined I would be able to ride Sherman when I went to see the land. Maybe, I thought, in just a few more days.

We heard a rattle and looked up to see Ike and the boys rolling into the yard in the wagon. Ike swung down and hopped over to join us.

"Good land," he boomed. "Got some water on it. Not as big a pond as this one, but it's got a little creek cutting through and a pond. We might even cut a path through the trees and hook up the properties. Got a couple good places to build a house, too. We need to build us a proper house and a barn. Then we'll get some cows." He gazed out at Diehl's cows, still grazing on Ike's property around the pond. "I'm gonna have to charge them some rent," he mumbled.

After a while, Ike struggled to his feet. "We need to go for a meeting with Hayes over at the bank," he announced.

The name sounded familiar, but I had to think for a minute. Oh yes, Mark Hayes was the president of the bank in town. I had dealt with him when I bought this land for Ike and his family. Julia stood and offered me a hand up. I stood, giving Ike a puzzled glance.

"Why am I going?" Julia slipped an arm around my waist and started me over toward the wagon.

Ike turned and shrugged. "I'm not real sure what it's about, myself," he said. "Hayes said he has some kind of proposal for us. Julia wants to come, and Jeanne said she wants you to go with us. That's all we have room for, unless somebody wants to ride in the back of the wagon. Hayes said you might want to be there. C'mon." He waved his hand toward the wagon. I climbed up with an effort and settled down for the ride.

We rolled into town, and to the surprise of all of us, Boone was waiting in front of the bank. "I'm joinin' you for the meeting," he informed us.

"You!" Ike stared at him. "How do you even know about the meeting?"

Boone drew himself up to his full height. "There wouldn't even be no meeting without me."

None of us had a response to that one, but Boone clearly couldn't keep from telling us more.

"You know, even bank presidents can get a little chatty when they've had a few beers," he said smugly.

It was my turn to stare at him. "You were buying beer for Mark Hayes?"

Boone looked injured. "I didn't say I was buyin' it. I was just drinking it with him. An' he felt like talking a little. An' I made a couple suggestions, that's all."

When it became clear he had told us all he was going to tell us, we went on into the bank and were shown into Hayes's office.

After only a few moments of talk about things in the town, Hayes got down to business.

"You know, I'm sure," he said, "that Virgil Diehl has abandoned his property. What you may not have known is that Mr. Diehl was severely behind in his payments to the bank. So far behind, in fact, that the bank would have taken legal action if it were not for a problem with the prior sheriff of this county. The prior sheriff, ah...shall we say, prevented us from taking action."

We exchanged a few glances around the table. We weren't sure exactly how Daniels had prevented the action, but Hayes didn't fill us in on that.

"What matters now," he concluded, "is that the bank has taken action and repossessed the property, as of last Friday."

Boone chortled. "What he means is that the bank done took it back," he put in helpfully.

A shadow of a smile crossed Hayes's face. "Thank you, Boone," he said. "That is exactly what it means."

Hayes picked up a few papers on his desk, read them briefly and then continued. "The bank doesn't really want a vacant property sitting out there, and there are few buyers around right now. Boone made a suggestion the other night. I'm ready to make a proposal to you, gentlemen, based on that suggestion. Here's what we're offering: There are maybe four hundred head of cattle on that land right now. Actually, they are grazing on your land now, Mr. Hawkins. They belonged to Virgil Diehl, but he is out of state, and if he returns, the Texas Rangers will charge him with murder for a shooting in Big Spring several years ago. Mr. Diehl seems to be permanently out of the picture."

Hayes paused for a sip of water. "The bank could probably make a legal claim on those cows, but that would take a while and it might be hard to prove ownership. We don't really want cattle, anyway. Mr. Diehl owed another $2,000 on that land, and we think it is probably worth more than $2,500 with the house and bunkhouse on the property. So, our offer to you is this: you take possession of the *wild cows* roaming on your land and give the bank $1,000 for them. In addition, we will sell you the Diehl property, including the house, for $2,500. We would need $500 in cash up front for the ranch. We would then assign Diehl's note to you, showing that you owe $2,000 to the bank. The total of $1,500 in cash would be due in thirty days."

Ike, Julia and I sat back, soaking in what we had just been told. Boone seemed to fiddle around in a bag he had brought in with him. Ike finally grabbed a piece of paper and a pencil. I could see he was doing some arithmetic over there. After a couple minutes, he picked up the paper and waved it around in the air. "Okay," he said, "there's about 130 steers out there and a few older cows I could sell and probably come up with $1,000. I'd hate to sell more, because we need the rest to start a herd and pay off that $2,000 on the note. We still need about $500 in cash and I don't have anymore." He looked over in my direction.

I leaned forward, thinking things over. "I have $200. I could pay you for the land we're on right now," I said. "That's most of what I have, but I'll have money coming in from the sheriff's job. You and your family can move to the house Diehl built, and I can take the cabin and the 130 acres I bought for you." I fell silent. "That still leaves us short by three hundred dollars," I began. Then I jumped suddenly at the loud thumping sound to my right. I spun around to look at Boone, who had just dropped a heavy burlap bag on the desk.

"I got three hunnerd in there," he declared. "I got more'n that, but you can have three hunnerd. I'm in."

The rest of us seemed to be speechless.

Boone swept his gaze around the room. "What, you didn't think I had any money? I been livin' for free in the saloon and drawin' pay for years. What'd you think I done with my money?"

"Well," I mumbled, "you haven't been buying me any beer with it."

Boone ignored my remark completely while Ike produced the paper and pencil again and began scratching down some numbers. "Boone," Ike thundered. "Glad to have you. You can own one-quarter of the herd for that three hundred dollars."

"Done," said Boone. He began counting three hundred dollars out of the bag on the desk.

Ike turned his gaze to me. "I'll be glad to sell you that land and the cabin for two hundred dollars," he told me. "As a matter of fact," he continued, turning to look at Julia, "if I'm reading these cards right, and you're a smart man, you'll wind up owning some of the ranch, too."

I looked over at Julia and read the twinkle in those eyes. "Don't worry," I told Ike. "I'm a very smart man."

As the others shook hands and stood up to go, I remained seated, staring through the window at the streets of Fredericksburg.

"A few months ago," I said, half to myself, "I was alone on a played-out piece of land, wondering what to do with myself. How did all this happen so fast?"

Julia leaned over and took my face in both her hands. She gave me a lingering kiss on the lips. "Don't you know, sweetie?" she asked. "It's McCabe's luck."

# A Look At Book Two
## McCabe's Law

**Some men follow the law—Jake McCabe lays it down.**

Jake McCabe didn't come to Fredericksburg looking for trouble. Fresh off a hard-won election and carrying the scars of war and old feuds, he hoped this quiet Texas town might finally offer a chance at peace. But peace is hard to come by on the frontier.

Water wars between ranchers are only the beginning. When Union renegades descend from the hills and chaos takes root, Jake finds himself outgunned and outmanned—and with his deputy laid up, he turns to the re-formed Texas Rangers for backup.

But nothing cuts deeper than what comes next. When the renegades take the woman Jake loves, the law becomes personal —and this time, justice wears a badge with McCabe's name on it.

### *AVAILABLE JULY 2025*

# About the Author

Patrick Lindsay came to Texas by way of Missouri, Canada, and California and has been proud to call the Lone Star State his home for more than forty years now. He retired in 2017 from "another life" as a CPA, whereafter he turned his hand to writing.

He has read just about everything by Louis L'Amour and first decided to give Western writing a try on his initial day of retirement. He has been writing ever since and loves the idea that so many people get enjoyment from his work.

Patrick and his wife Michelle live on a cattle ranch near Fort Worth along with cows, horses, chickens, and a very spoiled Great Pyrenees dog. He is an avid fan of the St. Louis Cardinals in baseball and the Kansas City Chiefs in football.